THE SAGE OF DIBBIN CREEK

D. DAUPHINEE

KICKING PIG
PRESS

This book is a work of fiction. While many of the main characters were real people, some were not. Conversations between characters (real or imagined) are a product of the author's imagination or are used fictitiously. Though the book is based on real events and people, any resemblance to actual persons, living or dead, events, or locals is entirely coincidental.

Illustrations are from the sketch books of
Alton Sands and Sam Candage,

www.ddauphinee.com

Book design by Cyrusfiction Productions

Printed in the United States of America

ISBN: 978-0-9863089-5-6 (Paperback)
ISBN: 978-0-9863089-6-3 (eBook)
ISBN: 978-0-9863089-7-0 (Hardcover)

Kicking Pig Press
P. O. Box 45, Bradley, ME 04411, U.S.A.

To Tim & Laurie Ashe
for being there.

CONTENTS

"Now I see the secret of the making of the best persons, It is to grow in the open air and to eat and sleep with the earth."

—Walt Whitman

One
THE FARM

"Tell me again, how my dad died?" I asked.

Mother was washing dishes. She looked up into the window over the kitchen sink and stared into the cold, pre-dawn blackness. Then she picked up a hand towel, turned to face me, and smiled. Though she was used to the questions in the seven years since my father passed away, I don't think it ever got any easier for her to hear them. With great patience, she would tell me about the tragedy, and each time I started the conversation the same way, "How did he die?"

It was the only way I knew to broach the topic.

The only real memories I had of that day were the blank look in my mother's eyes, visions of family members and friends sitting around the living room crying and blowing their noses, and my dad's friend Teri holding me tightly when all I wanted to do was run outside.

Mom looked at me. She smiled, sighed, and dried her hands. She slid into a kitchen chair beside me and massaged my shoulder.

"Well, Sam, you were only five. Your daddy was working the fields. He was working very hard for the family when something went wrong, and the tractor he was driving rolled over on top of him." She paused, then she continued, "He died very quickly. And it's important you know that he was a good man and loved you more than anything."

I nodded slightly and tried to smile. The story had stayed the same.

Mom smiled back at me and asked, "Is there anything else you want to know about him? I know we've talked about him often, but I like it when you want to hear the stories."

I hadn't planned any other questions but thought briefly and said, "Was he a good farmer?"

"Oh, he was an excellent farmer. You know, people still say he grew the best pumpkins and sweet corn around."

"Your dad was an interesting man," she continued. "Let's see; he loved to read, and he loved the woods, the wild animals, and the creeks—just like you. He loved to fish, and you already know he was a mountaineer. But most of all, he loved his son."

I gave her a look that must've said I wanted to hear more.

So, she told me more. "Besides the family and the farm, your dad loved to walk in the forests. I see a lot of him in you and it breaks my heart when I think of all the fun you two would've had together."

Mom never held back in raising me. I had been dealt a harsh blow, losing my father when so young, and I suppose she knew that I'd figure out a lot on my own regardless of what she told me. My father had died, and that was the truth of it. I would, just like my mom, have to deal with it. Ours was a small world out there on the farm. Since no other kids my age lived nearby, she was my mother, my acting father, and my friend.

There aren't many certainties on farms, except that it is certain the sun, the wind, cold, heat, insects, and the invisible spores of mold that are everywhere always will try to put us out of business. That's the way farming has always been. But through the years, there was another certainty I could count on; I made sure Mom knew I loved her, and I always felt she found great happiness in that. From me, as a small, loving boy, she found some peace.

When she could think of nothing else to say, she sat with bent elbow, her chin in one hand, and combed the fingers of her other hand through my hair. I remember speaking up as though experiencing a brand-new idea: "Can I go fishing tomorrow?"

She gave me a funny look. "Honey, you go fishing every Saturday and every Sunday. Why should tomorrow be any different?"

"I don't always fish."

"No?"

"No. Sometimes I just explore. I look for animal tracks, arrowheads, garter snakes, and bugs. And sometimes I pretend I'm Meriweather Lewis, or Daniel Boone, sneaking through the thickets, out of sight of the Indians."

Mom looked at me. I often overheard her tell her best friend, Teri, that she wished I had a playmate.

"Of course," I continued, "the Indians weren't the bad guys. This was their land. And down where the creek flows into the river? I bet they had a village right there. Remember? That's where we found those arrowheads." I often imagined I was one of them, living in their village, hunting, fishing, and living off the land. I spent hours looking at my father's books about animals, birds, and local Indian tribes. He had a *lot* of books.

"I think I'm caught up with the planting schedule." She glanced at the calendar next to the fridge; April 16, 1972. "You can fish after you do your homework *if* you remember the rules."

"Yes, yes," I said, "I have to stay between the big maple trees where you can see me. You know, Mom, if you could come with me, there's a much better chance for trout upstream from the maples. In that whole stretch where you can see me, there's only chubs." Like most fishermen, I regarded chubs as a kind of trash fish.

She smiled at me. "There *are* only chubs—not *there is* only chubs."

"I'll try," she replied. "Maybe in the afternoon." She knew *her* chores on the farm were never done.

I was glad when I saw our friend Teri climbing the porch steps. She always made me happy, even when she slapped my shoulder, which she always did when she was excited about something.

"Hola!" Teri breezed through the back door and into the kitchen. For a long time, I thought she was my aunt. It would be years before I realized she wasn't related to us. Teri was my dad's best friend before he and my mom were married, and after he died, she became my mom's closest friend. I think Teri was at our farm more than at her own house. She helped us with the chores and the farmwork a *lot*. Teri was also an excellent artist, painting landscapes and nature scenes in both pastels and watercolors.

She dropped some groceries onto the kitchen table, kissed me on my head, and sat beside me.

"You guys look serious," she said.

"I was just asking Mom about my dad again."

Teri glanced at Mom leaning against the sink, then smiled back at me and rubbed my shoulder. "You know what I still love about your father?" she asked.

Before I could answer, she kept going.

"I love that he's still here, in you, shining his love on us every day."

Teri had beautiful, wavy red hair—always tied either into a ponytail or pulled back with a headband—and she had a lovely smile with big dimples, and she always made me feel good. Sometimes, I felt better just knowing she would be coming to the farm. We three did everything together: Thanksgiving and Christmas dinners, school events, and birthdays. Sometimes, Teri would go to the creek with me and paint with her pastels while I fished.

I grinned up at her, and Teri sat back in her chair. Her eyes opened wide, and she said, "Who'll help me bake some muffins?"

Mom returned to the sink and stared out the window through the early morning light at the little creek meandering along the far side of the field and at the tall maples and spruce trees that grew next to it. She looked very tired.

Two

The Creek — My Respite

It was two o'clock in the afternoon before I finished my chores. It was early May, planting time, and planting seeds was one of the few chores on the farm I did not mind. I liked poking the tall stick through the black plastic mulch stretched over each row in the field. I would tear a small hole in it and, from the pouch hanging at my waist, drop at least two pumpkin seeds into the little dent in the soil beneath the plastic. Then, before taking a long, exaggerated step and starting the process again, I would tap the little hole with the stick to cover the seeds with a bit of soil. I always worried the seeds wouldn't have time to take root before the crows ate them.

When I was finished planting, I grabbed my fishing rod from the pantry, heard the screen door bang shut behind me, and walked through the thickets along one of the paths that led from the crop fields down to the creek. I had to be careful not to catch the line of my fishing rod on the twigs and branches or on the raspberry thorns that tried to snag my blue jeans. When I approached the brook, I stopped and looked through the tree branches for any rising fish. That creek was my happy place.

I brushed aside a sweet-smelling, low-hanging cedar bough and looked around. Ostrich fern grew thick and heavy in the low, damp places along the stream. Wild, pretty, and delicate purple violets stood at attention on the banks where streaking columns of sunlight bore down through the tall pines and cedars. In the muddy banks, I saw deer tracks and the handlike pattern of the raccoon's footprints. There was a smooth, flat rock with some muskrat droppings. I spotted a sandpiper balancing unsteadily, teetering among the wet rocks, swaying back and forth like a drunken sailor as it searched for insects. Thirty feet above the creek, a kingfisher sat patiently on a cedar branch that overhung the banks. It rested poised and ready to plunge head-first into the pool as it watched a dragonfly dart in and out of the shadows hunting mosquitos and blackflies.

A creek harbors a host of living things who call it home: turtles, frogs, mayflies, and water bugs live in it. Trout, chub, dace, and minnows share the watery world with beavers, mink, and the muskrat. Deer come down at dusk and dawn to drink. The raccoon patrols the water's edge at night, searching for freshwater clams and crayfish. Each creek is an aquatic biome teeming with life, and if one pays attention, it offers lessons in biology—which is life.

By the time I had finished watching all the living things along the creek, it was time to head home for supper. I hadn't even fished! But I didn't mind; I fished the creek almost every day.

My favorite times to be on the creek were mornings or late afternoons. I liked the extended, cool shadows of dawn and dusk when the sunlight intensified, and in the deep pools, fish could often be seen rising for insects. Sometimes, I would watch the fish make dozens of dimpling rises up and down the creek, each sending tiny ripples in the otherwise calm water. Other times, I would see fish jumping in the faster runs of rapids and riffles where the creek plunges toward its meeting place with the big river. Those rises were different; the fish splashed in the current, and occasionally small chub and trout would come clear out of the water. I tried to fish for them but usually caught nothing. Those trout just didn't want the worm on my hook. But when the fish weren't rising for insects in a frenzy, I could always catch at least a couple of chubs with my bait.

When it was too hot to fish, or if they weren't biting, I usually explored the creek's banks. The edges of the creek were crowded with alders, cedars, and fern. Behind them were tall stands of birch, white pine, oaks, maples, and occasionally some wild cherry, which didn't grow very tall. In the small, shallow coves made by the inside bends of the meandering creek grew mounds of elderberry, dogtooth violets, and water lilies.

I would walk through the woods, pretending I was an important explorer. Near the creek, I would search for arrowheads. Farther into the woods, I would look for animal tracks or scat. I carried a few field guides in a small backpack, and whenever I found something I couldn't identify, I'd look it up right then and there. I could not read well at that age, but I loved books.

I was always amazed at how many different species of birds I saw near the creek or at the edge of our fields. One day, as I walked home and climbed over the old stone wall that separated the forest and one of our pumpkin fields, something swooped by my face quite fast. I looked up to see two swallows darting around close to the fallow field. They were a darker blue than the swallows that nested in our barn, and their bellies looked creamy white. They were catching insects. I leaned back against the stone wall and studied them. They began to rise higher into the sky and swoop in tight loops, one circling above the other and then diving below. I thought it was a mating ceremony. But after a while, I saw something fall from the sky. The more I watched, the more curious I became; I was convinced they were playing with a small white feather. One would fly high above its mate and drop the feather. As it fell to earth, the second bird would dive down and catch it in its tiny beak, then soar higher and repeat the process, dropping it to the first bird. They were playing catch.

I thought I was witnessing something quite unusual and was privileged to see birds playing. I read about them in the Sibley Guide to Birds as soon as I got home. Apparently, the feather game I saw above the fallow field wasn't so unusual. But I thought it was pretty cool, and tree swallows became one of my favorite birds. For years, I would watch the swift birds work a field, whether playing with feathers or feasting on insects.

Those swallows did not know it, but they steered me onto a life-long path of observing and loving birds.

Three
PLANTING TIME

A few weeks after our conversation in the kitchen, Mom accompanied me to the creek to fish. She had loved to fish ever since she was a little girl, but she was usually too busy with the farm and her job. I was happy she finally found the time to go.

We shared my rod, taking turns flipping the swivel, spinner, and worm into likely spots. I pushed her to go farther up the creek, far upstream from where I was allowed to go alone. She seemed pleased to hike through the woods upstream. I think she was just happy to be out of the house or barn and not working one of the fields. I was happy to have some company. So many times, week in and week out, I had to fish alone. Teri often said my playing alone so much was why I daydreamed as often as I did. Mom worried I daydreamed too much, but Teri suggested it might make me an artist someday. I don't know about any of that; I just loved to fish.

We went as far upstream as her time allowed. We stepped up to the creek bank when she figured we'd hiked far enough. Here, instead of the water flowing flat and quietly between the fields, it was tumbling and winding around hundreds of boulders. Each twist in the creek's course created a bend pool where the current slowed and the water deepened. On the far side of each pool, there was an undercut bank shaded by an overhanging cedar or fir tree. Here, I knew, was where trout would be.

I let Mom go first. It was fun to see her doing something, *anything* for fun. It had been a while since she had casted a line, but she knew what to do. She flipped open the wire bail of her reel and flicked the worm into the dark pool. Almost the instant it hit the water, her rod tip bent, and the line darted left and right and turned in little jittery circles. She didn't say a word, but the smile on her face told the story. She reeled as she stepped back, pulling the fish closer to us and into the shallow water. The animal thrashed and splashed as Mom lifted it onto the mossy bank. I knew from experience that fish would sometimes spit loose the hook just when you think you've got it and flop back into the water. I hurried and grabbed the writhing thing as it flipped and somersaulted in the moss, and I held up a pretty, seven-inch brook trout. Its back was dark and covered with red and yellow spots with blueish halos, but it had a pure white belly. Its fins were a dark orange-red except for a stark white strip along the front, and its brown, almost black back was marked with a lighter brown worm-like pattern covering the big dorsal fin. It was beautiful.

Mom handed me the rod to take a turn, but I pushed it back into her hands. It was fun enough for me to watch *her* enjoying herself. My Mother didn't have many opportunities to go fishing with me, but I was very happy when she did, as much for her as for myself. She caught two more about the same size from the same pool. I knew the legal size limit trout was six inches, so we kept them for the frying pan. While she fished, I cut a small, forked branch off an alder using my father's Old Timer pocketknife. I trimmed off all the leaves and whittled it into a fork about a foot-and-a-half long. I picked up the trout and inserted the long section of the fork up through its gills and out through the mouth. The fish slid down the stick and was caught in the fork. I did that with all the trout and ended up with a nice little stringer of fish, easily carried. I'm not crazy about eating fish—just catching them—but my mother loves trout. We took turns fishing other likely pools on the way back to the farm, and though we caught quite a few, we ended up keeping only six to eat. We could have legally kept more but didn't need them, so back into the creek most of them went.

When we finally returned to the calm water that flows next to the crop fields, I was left at the edge of the creek to clean the trout. I watched Mom walk across the field, hopping over each planted row and back to the house. I had always been told she was athletic as a teenage girl, and now, at thirty-five, she was still fit and agile.

I again pulled my dad's old pocketknife from my jeans, opened it, and ran my thumb along the blade. It felt sharp enough. One by one, I slid the fish off the stringer stick and, as my mom taught me, held the fish belly-side up with its head pointing away from me. I slit the trout from anus to throat. I carefully used only the blade's tip, making the cut shallow. You can cut into the innards if you go too deep with the knife. You don't want to do that. The gross stuff that's in the intestines can ruin the beautiful pink flesh of the fish. I then cut a slit between the two gills under the fish's "chin."

Once cut open, I pried open the body with my fingers. I held the fish by its jaw with one hand and grasped the gills with the other. I pulled firmly on the gills and removed them along with the slimy guts. Easy-peasy.

I was always amazed the fish guts don't have a particular smell, or I'm not sure I could've handled cleaning the fish. I tossed the innards and gills into the creek for the turtles and swished the fish back and forth underwater to rinse out the body cavity. Then, it was my turn to hop across the planted fields and return home. I stopped to look for birds working the fields hunting insects but saw none. I started walking again. It was a good leap for me to jump clear across the planted rows. Mom had made it look easy.

When we planted pumpkins, we would drag a big roll of thin, black plastic mulch behind the tractor on an attachment that would unroll, stretch, and bury the edges with dirt — all in one motion! The plastic mulch kept the soil beneath warm during cool spring days, which helped the seeds germinate, and also, no weeds could grow under the plastic. It worked great for growing pumpkins, but pulling up the plastic after harvest time and getting rid of it was the dirtiest, worst job on the farm. If we had a good year and sold enough pumpkins to cover the upcoming winter's heating oil, Mom would pay a couple of teenagers from Milton to help with it. But most years, it was just me, Mom, and Teri, and I hated doing it.

Later, Mom rolled each trout in cornmeal and fried them in bacon grease and a bit of butter with salt and pepper. "The trick," she told me, "is to cook them slowly—simmer them patiently."

I ate one small trout with some scrambled eggs, but she ate the other five with nothing else. Mom loved eating fish and seafood, too, but we almost never had any. It was too expensive.

After breakfast, I took some books onto the porch and looked through every one I could find about brook trout.

Four

GIVE ME SHELTER

When summer break from school arrived, the fields had already been planted each year. The corn, pumpkins, squash, and cucumbers were already sprouted and growing. The pepper and tomato seedlings would have been transplanted from the large greenhouse into the gardens. Even though there were many farm chores to do every day, summer meant more time to explore the woods and to fish.

That summer, I turned twelve, and I did two things that I hadn't previously done: I tried to learn how to hunt small animals, and I learned how to build shelters in the woods. I hunted with a homemade bow and arrow. The bow was made of an alder branch with the bark peeled off, and the arrows were cut from the straight reeds that grow along the lower part of the creek. I collected the feathers around the barnyard and glued and tied them on with some of Mom's sewing thread. I had no arrowheads; the arrow tips were whittled to a sharp point. I think I only scared and annoyed the partridge that pecked the ground under the cedar and spruce trees and the rabbits I shot at along the edge of the fields. I was a bad shot. After a while, it seemed like the rabbits came to think of the whole thing as some sort of game. I suppose it was just as well. If I had killed or trapped anything, Mom would have made me clean, cook, and eat it, no matter what it was. The only animals I think I had a good chance to kill were the dreaded groundhogs who lived under our barn and terrorized our gardens. The thought of Mom making me eat a groundhog soured me on hunting, and eventually, I stuck to fishing and observing the forest and everything that lived in it.

Sometimes, in the midday heat, I would lie next to the creek in the shade of the cedars and imagine I was living alone in the forest full time, on my own entirely. In that world, I could hunt with bow and arrow, trap small animals. I even imagined building a deadfall trap big enough to kill a deer, and fishing with homemade hooks.

Armed with only a hatchet and a knife, I would build a tiny log cabin and live there. I would live by my wits. The only problem with the plan was that I didn't think I had any wits. Not really. Maybe I knew a little about the forest, but I also knew that book-smart people have starved to death in the wild.

Other times, I imagined I lived in an earlier time, before the arrival of the white man, and had been part of an Indian tribe. I would daydream for hours about how that would be, living in peace and learning their clever ways of living off the land.

At the school library, I tried to read the books I found about the forest and the animals that dwelt in it. Then in an old box in our barn, I found a dirty and dusty and tattered Boy Scouts of America manual dated 1965. I looked at the drawings in it and was captivated by the chapter on shelter building. Several simple shelters were illustrated; most were constructed by lashing sticks and tree limbs together. The illustrations helped me figure out some of the words, and with a pencil I circled, '… *the Adirondack, the Scout, the Pioneer, the Tepee,* and *the Wickiup.*' The only word I could sound out was the tepee, which I had seen many times in old Western movies. That night, I decided to find a hidden place in the woods and build one of each, starting with the Adirondack. I did not understand some of the instructions, but the detailed drawings would be enough for me to build the shelters.

On the first of May, I dragged down to the creek a red, rusty Radio Flyer wagon loaded with things I could find in the barn: baling string and wire, a hatchet that was badly in need of sharpening, and a small hand saw which I learned later was used to cut keyholes in wooden doors.

It wasn't easy pulling the wagon through the forest, and a few times, I had to lift it over fallen logs or moss-covered boulders on which it was hard to find sound footing. It was my first time to the creek in months without my fishing rod.

I eventually found what I thought would be a good spot for a shelter. It was about thirty yards from the creek and between the big maples, in a little clearing that had a relatively flat place for the construction.

The Adirondack shelter is a lean-to that is open in the front, and the sides can be left open or closed off. I wanted to be able to close my shelter off when necessary to keep the wind from whipping through. Directly in front of the shelter site were two good-sized boulders rounded off on top. They would make good seats. I imagined sitting in my future shelter, watching the goings-on down at the creek. I parked the wagon, picked up the hatchet, and started looking for some small spruce trees that could be cut to a length of about five feet. Both small logs needed to have a "crotch" at the top — these would be the first two vertical poles. Maybe I was too picky because it took me nearly an hour to find the perfect poles, limb them, and trim the top branches to make a crotch at the top. I then lay on my back on the flat spot, reached above my head with a stick, and scratched a line on the forest floor. Then I did a sit-up and marked another line beyond my feet. This was the length I wanted for the shelter. Then, using the blunt end of the hatchet like a hammer, I drove the sharpened butt ends of the two crotched poles into the marked lines. They stayed standing. It looked like about a seven-foot cross piece was needed to place in the two crotches. I quickly found one, cut it down, and laid it across the crotches. I couldn't get the vertical poles very far into the ground but they stayed standing long enough for me to lash the three poles together with baling twine. At first, I couldn't figure out how to know the length of the poles of the roof that would angle up and rest against the crosspiece. Then I remembered reading that in the olden days people used string or ropes to measure things when they built their homes and temples. So, I tied the end of the baling twine to one of the crotched, vertical poles and unwound the spool to the second marked line where I wanted the back of the lean-to to rest on the ground. I added one arm's length to the string and cut it. This length of string would serve as my yardstick.

I cut six thin saplings using the measuring string, knocked all the branches and twigs off with the hatchet, and dragged them to the shelter. (The Scout manual showed a drawing using four slanting poles for the back wall, but I thought mine needed six.) I leaned them against the crosspiece and tied each one with twine. The length was perfect; they overhung the crosspiece at the top by more than a foot. It was quickly looking like a structure! I had been at it for a few hours and decided to quit in time to get back for supper.

Back at the house, my hands were covered in pitch and sap, but I managed to get most of it off with the garden hose before Mom saw it. I don't know why I was worried … I was always covered in something. We didn't have money for new clothes, and I believe each day I came home when my clothes weren't ruined my mother thought of as a victory. Mine was a busy life, always outside in the forest and fields, but I tried to be careful with my clothes.

In the morning, my farm chores consisted of watering the hundreds of plants in the greenhouse and filling pots with soil. Mother would plant seedlings into the pots, which would later be transplanted *again* into hanging baskets. She made beautiful baskets which she sold in our little farm stand that stood at the end of our driveway. Any extra flower baskets she would sell to the hardware store in Milton for half-price. It was all fun work, and I didn't mind it. Once the chores were finished, I returned to the creek, pulling the red wagon with all my shelter-building supplies.

I half suspected the shelter might have fallen during the night, but there it was, just as I'd left it. I went straight to work, collecting balsam boughs. I was careful to snap off only the thicker, heavier branches because every November Mother and I would collect the small tips of the youngest boughs to make Christmas wreaths. We sold those in the farm stand also. That's how we got money for Christmas gifts.

Once I harvested as many boughs as I could carry, I placed them on the slanting roof of the shelter. I tied the top two rows of branches to the poles with baling twine, the rest I could weave together. After quite a few trips, I had a nice thick roof and sidewalls, and the shelter was finished, except for the bedding. I collected more boughs for that, but this time from spruce trees (we didn't use spruce for the Christmas wreaths—only balsam) which meant I could snap off the tiniest, softest branch tips. I did not want any sharp branches under my bed. Once the shelter floor was covered with about six inches of spruce tips, I covered it with an old wool horse blanket I had found in the barn. It was quite comfortable!

I was proud of my first attempt at building something, and as I lay on that blanket I imagined a hearth made of river rocks and a crackling fire. I had had no help, and as far as I was concerned, it was a fine shelter.

The next thing I knew, I awoke from a nice nap. I looked at my watch. Lunchtime! I ran back to the house. I would return to my new home away from home to retrieve my wagon in the afternoon.

Five

WHAT APPROACHES IN THE WOODS?

Over lunch, I told my mother all about my shelter next to the creek. She seemed impressed and asked to see it later in the day.

"How did you learn to build it?" she asked.

"From that old scouting handbook I found in the barn."

She smiled at me. I think she was proud, also.

After supper, we walked across the bottom field, stepped over the old stone wall, and picked our way through the woods toward the creek. I was excited for her to see what I'd made.

As we walked into the clearing, I looked at her face. Her eyes widened, and I could see she was surprised at how good the shelter looked. I had made sure the clearing was cleaned up. Mother walked around all four sides of the lean-to. She felt the chopped end of one of the poles. She looked into the red wagon parked behind the shelter and then she sat down on the bedding. She ran her hand over the grey-and-red horse blanket, then leaned down and smelled it.

"Smells like the barn," she smiled. "That's nice." I liked that my mother was different from most moms.

"Sam, honey," she said, "You did a wonderful job."

"Thanks, Mom. Do you think I could spend a night here?"

She looked around the clearing. She got up, being careful not to bump her head on the overhanging poles that carried the spruce boughs. Again, she walked around the little clearing. She found a soft, mossy flat spot about thirty feet from my shelter and sat down.

"I think you should," she replied, "but I'd like to be with you. I can pitch your dad's old mountaineering tent here. That way, if it starts to rain and the shelter leaks too much, you can pile in with me. How's that sound?"

"Perfect!" I said. I had been asking to go camping for a while, but we couldn't find the time to be away from the farm. *What could be better?* I thought. *We'll be camping, we'll still be at the farm for morning chores, and I'll get to be in my very own shelter. Why didn't I think of this before?*

"Tomorrow is Saturday," said Mom. "Let's do it then."

As we walked back to the house pulling the wagon, she said pensively, "If you're going to use that old hatchet, you must be *very* careful."

"I will," I replied.

She shook her head. "No, if you want to use the hatchet for things like shelter-building, I want to give you some lessons before you use it again. Deal?"

"Deal."

"First thing we will do," she said, "is I'll teach you how to sharpen it. Most accidents with hatchets or axes occur because the tools are dull. We have a grindstone in the barn. I'll teach you how to hone a nice sharp edge. That thing looks as dull as a hoe."

We did camp together the next night, and it is one of my favorite memories. While putting tent poles together and erecting her tent, she told me stories about my dad I had not heard.

"When I met your father," she said, "he was an accomplished mountaineer. Even did some guiding before we were married."

I had seen pictures of him standing in snow fields with tents all around him.

Kneeling, Mother snaked the thin poles through sleeves in the nylon tent as it lay flat on the ground. Then she sat back on her calves. "This tent … we used it on our honeymoon—the week after our wedding day."

She looked like she had eaten something very sour. Then she breathed heavily and smiled at me.

"You know, when we first bought this farm, your dad and I used to walk down here to this very spot. We would fish or just sit here in the springtime and watch the fish rise."

She turned her head toward the creek, then back to me.

"We said someday we would build a little log cabin here. It would be a quiet place for him to write, and it would also be a studio for me." She lay back and folded her hands behind her head. She gazed up at the stars glittering through the black tree branches. "I had big plans to get into stained glass. But then the accident happened, and I got too busy trying to keep the farm going—and raising a little man!"

I lay back and stared up through the web of black branches at the shadowy darkness and tried to focus on the sparkling stars in the nighttime sky.

After a couple of hours, my bedding wasn't as comfortable as I had hoped, but I didn't mind. As I watched the little campfire we had made burn down to embers, I became too warm in my father's old sleeping bag. As I pulled open the zipper of the bag, I could hear Mom faintly sniffing and breathing hard in her tent. When I realized she was crying, I stared back at the glowing, orange coals in the hearth and tried to think about the s'mores we had made earlier, the songs we sang around the campfire, and the stories she told of her childhood. Mother rarely cried. With her part-time job at the dentist's office, the running of the farm, and raising me, I don't think she had the time to cry very often.

In the morning, as we packed up, Mother said, "Teri would've loved being here last night, but I'm glad it was just the two of us this first time."

First time? Maybe she'll want to camp here again.

We pulled the red wagon home and started our farm chores.

Over the next month, I built more shelters using as a guide the illustrations in the scouting handbook. A short distance from my first shelter—the Adirondack—I built smaller structures called the "Scout," the "Pioneer," and the "Bark Teepee." I got better with each project. My little forest along the creek was beginning to look like a village. Having a sharp hatchet really helped, and it did feel safer to use. I felt I was becoming more experienced at woodscraft. I was confident of that. Mom explained that when honing the axe's cutting edge it should be precisely in line with the point in the center of the butt end of the handle, not sharpened or filed more on one side than the other. She told me never to use an axe when its head is loose and in danger of flying off the handle, then she showed me how to tighten the head with wooden or metal wedges. She explained that I should never leave it lying on the ground with the blade unprotected. She said I shouldn't use a good axe or hatchet to cut roots or sticks lying flat on the ground and showed me how to carry the tool safely.

That same weekend, we built an outdoor fire pit in the backyard. There, she could keep an eye on me as I learned the art of fire-building. I didn't get very good at it and went through several boxes of matches, but I was confident I could get a fire going if necessary without starting a forest fire. That was the important thing. I vowed to get better at building fires and keeping one going.

One afternoon while fishing and catching nothing but chubs, a giant eel came swimming upstream. I stared at it... *What a strange creature.* I didn't know anything about them and started wondering things like what they eat and why were they shaped so strangely. I leaned against a giant boulder and watched the eel slowly slither up to the head of the pool and disappear. I heard a blue jay scream and a chickadee call out from somewhere behind me, and a red squirrel in the cedar overhead began chattering, scolding me for being so bold to be sitting under her tree.

Suddenly, all the sounds ceased. I looked up. The squirrel was gone. I had already spent so long in the woods that I too sensed something and cocked an ear. Something, or someone, was stirring—a fox? A bobcat, maybe? A person? My mind started to race. A...*coyote*?! I don't know why I was afraid of coyotes, they don't actually bother people, but still, I was fearful of them. Something prompted the red squirrel and the Jay to sound an alarm, and every creature paused. The woods became deathly quiet. I sat extremely still and listened.

I looked around and spotted the red squirrel on a branch higher up. She was sitting hunchbacked and on full alert. Her tail, bushier than before, was folded up its back and curled over like the whisp of a ponytail. She, too, sat very still.

I heard footsteps and the undergrowth brush against something moving through the woods.

It was a man.

Six

I SEE FLY FISHING FOR THE FIRST TIME

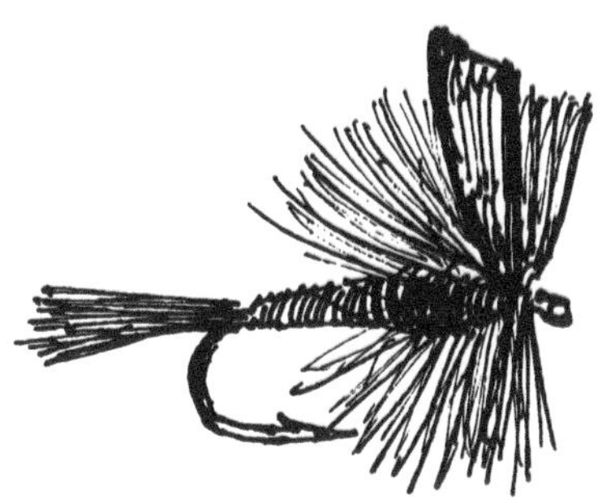

The man was old but tall and lean. He walked through the brush slowly and confidently, like a much younger man. The man was watching the creek more than where he was stepping. On second thought, he was somehow watching both the water and the ground simultaneously. He wore an antique pocketed vest made of brown canvas and carried a fishing rod. He had not seen me.

I had seen the man before, walking along the riverwalk in town. In the small village of Milton, he was the only man you'd see walking around town with a fishing rod, at least that I knew of. Now, watching him through the leaves, it occurred to me that even though I had seen him many times. I knew nothing about him and although everyone had likely seen him walking with his fishing rod, he had never come up in conversations at our house.

The man stepped up to some alders growing close to the creek at the tail of the pool, and I began to wonder what to do; if I waited till he got close, I might startle him to death! He could have a heart attack or something, and I sure didn't want to deal with that.

The old fisherman watched the pool, then bent down and inspected some of the leaves of the alders. Then, oddly, he gently shook the branches and looked around. *He must be looking for bugs*, I thought.

He crouched slightly and stepped closer to the edge of the creek. He took off his battered hat, examined it carefully, and pulled something from the hatband. He then pulled some line from the reel and snaked it through each guide on his rod and tied whatever he had pulled from his hat to the end of the line. He flipped the line into the water, let out some more line, and raised the rod tip high before quickly dropping the rod tip upstream toward the head of the pool. The line shot out the rod's guides across the pool, where it gently unfolded and dropped the tiny lure into the riffles without so much as a ripple. *How did he do that?* I had never seen fishing like that before.

I watched from fifty feet away as the old man held his rod tip high. His eyes followed the line as it slowly floated with the current. He kept most of the line out of the water. I couldn't see what happened, but suddenly, though gently he raised his rod tip and had a fish on. I could not believe it ... I could see by the square tail that it was a fat trout! We were between the big maples; this was not a stretch of the creek with trout in it. There were supposed to be only chubs here. That's all I ever caught this far downstream. After landing it, he bent down and returned the trout to the depths. I was amazed.

I could not take another minute of being undetected. As the old man prepared to make another cast, I whistled. The fellow twitched and looked in my direction. I waved sheepishly, and once he collected himself, he smiled and nodded back. *No heart attack*, I thought. The angler waved me over, and instead of making a second cast, he sat on a moss-covered boulder. I wound my way through the fern and alders to him and sat down.

"I was just sitting, daydreaming when you walked up the creek," I told him. "Didn't want to startle you."

"That's mighty considerate," he replied. He patted his chest and smiled. "If I'd walked up onto you, I'm not sure my ticker could've handled it."

I wanted to say, "*That's what I was thinking,*" but I just grinned at him instead.

The man reached toward me, extending his hand. "I'm Mr. Sands." As he said the words, he shook his head once as though he had caught himself. "Alton," he said, "Alton Sands. You may call me whatever you like."

I shook his hand shyly. "Samuel Candage. You can call me Sam. Everybody does."

"Pleased to meet you, Sam. Are you fishing? Have I stolen your water?"

I did not know what he meant by that. I shook my head. "I'm usually fishing, but not this time. Like I said … daydreaming."

The old man nodded and looked around. "Candage," he said. "You're from the farm through the woods?"

"That's right," I said.

"Well," replied Mr. Sands. "If you live on a farm, I think you're entitled to all the daydreaming you can find time for."

Again, those were my thoughts exactly.

"Mr. Sands," I said, "I've never seen fishing like that before."

"Oh," he replied, "this is fly fishing. It's a bit different from the way most kids around here fish."

I was staring at his fishing rod and its tiny reel. It looked like the rods in my father's den that Mother would never let me have. "*You don't know how to use those,*" she would always say.

"Wow," I said, "you caught a trout. I've never caught a trout down here, only chubs."

"Yes, that was probably lucky." Mr. Sands noticed my fishing rod leaning against a tree.

"You see, Sam, "fish aren't always eating angleworms. In fact, they hardly ever do." He opened a box of dozens of little fake flies on hooks. "Don't you think it might be better to offer trout what they normally eat?" He looked back at the creek. "To tell the truth, I didn't expect much from this pool."

I wanted to ask him how to fish that way — how to fly fish. I wanted to ask if it was difficult and if he thought I was old enough to learn it, but instead, I only nodded at his remark.

"Mr. Sands," I asked, "would it be okay if I watched you fish?"

He smiled at me. "I don't mind at all."

With that, he made a few more casts into the pool. I sat back far enough to stay out of his way. He had what seemed to be bites a couple of times but missed the fish. He did catch a few chubs, but he did not catch any more trout.

Mr. Sands fished from the bottom of the pool upstream to the head. After a dozen casts, he reeled in his line, turned, and waved at me. Then he walked up the creek seeking new water to try. That was it. He passed beyond the big maple, where I could not follow, though I wanted to. I wanted to watch him cast his fly; it was much prettier than when I used my worm and spin-fishing rod. I walked as far as the big maple to try to see him, but he had disappeared into the alders that grow thick next to the stream.

That evening, I approached Mother in the kitchen. She was doing the dishes again. I picked up a dish towel to dry the plates for her.

"So," I said, "I was wondering if I could have Dad's old fly-fishing rods in his office?"

Mother stopped scrubbing a bowl and looked up at the window. It was dark outside, and all she could see was her reflection. But she stared past the reflection and through the window anyway.

"Do you know about fly fishing?" she asked.

"Not really, but I've seen it. Today, down at the creek. Mister … Mister …" *I had forgotten his name already! How could I have done that?*

"Mister … Albert, or Alfred something," I said.

Mother turned and looked at me. "You saw another fisherman? And you spoke to him?"

"Yes. He had a nice face, and he could really fish."

"You remember what I've told you about talking to strangers?" she asked.

"I'm not supposed to," I said sheepishly. "But I kinda had to say *something*. He walked near where I was sitting, and he didn't see me. I was worried if I didn't say something, he might get a heart attack."

Mother nodded. "I can see that. But I hope you didn't bother him. I know you get lonely for someone other than just me to talk to."

"I didn't. He fished upstream, past the big maple, so I watched him casting until he was out of sight. I liked the way it looked, it was sort of, I dunno, pretty."

"Yes, it is pretty," she said. "Okay, Honey. We'll talk about your dad's fly-fishing equipment later. I could show you some very basic things about casting that your dad taught me, but you'll need proper lessons before you use any of it. We'll figure it out."

After we finished the dishes, we both went to the living room and Mother picked-up where she had left off reading aloud *Charlotte's Web*. (That was my favorite book, and it was one that I could read nearly on my own. Mother often said I had memorized the whole book.) I lay on my back on the floor with my hands behind my head and listened to every word. After an hour, we stopped for the night, just as Templeton was returning with the goose egg, and I said, "You know, I also have Teri to talk to when she's here."

Mother smiled at me over the top of the book. She loved her best friend, Teri, and she knew that without her in our lives, things would be much harder.

"Besides," I said, "I'd rather talk to you than with anyone else."

She blew me a kiss.

I couldn't wait to learn to fish like the old man at the creek.

Seven

I Meet the Old Man a Second Time

I didn't get my fly fishing lesson the next day, or the following week, or the week after that. I did find a book at the Milton library that, using drawings, teaches the reader to cast a fly rod, but it only confused me. Three weeks after I first spoke with Mother about my dad's fly fishing equipment, I was having fun catching chubs with my spinning rod in the little pool in front of my shelter, only fifty yards from where I had watched the old man catch a trout in that most unlikely spot.

It was a beautiful summer day, sunny and not too hot or muggy. I was catching chubs on almost every cast, and a few of them were huge, maybe a half-pound each. I was just about to cast my spinnerbait when I heard a twig snap behind me. It was the old man! When I turned and waved, he smiled and said, "Hello, Sam. Today, it's my turn not to startle *you* to death!"

I reeled my line in and walked over to him. I must have looked sheepish as if I was searching for what to say.

"It's Alton Sands," he said with a wink.

I was embarrassed about forgetting his name and wanted to apologize, but I was rattled and stuck doggedly to the re-introduction. "Sam Candage."

"I remember, Sam. How's the fishing?'

"Just chubs. My mom doesn't let me go farther than the big maple upstream, and all there is down here are these darned chubs."

Mr. Sands looked at me like he wanted to tell me something, then turned toward the pool I had been fishing. I turned toward him. "You caught a trout down here; I watched you catch it. But chubs are all I ever catch."

"Well," Mr. Sands replied, "that was almost a month ago. The water has warmed up a lot since then."

I understood what he said but looked at him, hoping for more information. It must have been obvious to the old man.

"Do you know about trout and how they're different from chubs?

Before I could answer, he said, "Chubs. Their real name is fallfish, by the way."

I wanted to say something, to show Mr. Sands I knew a little something about fishing, but I couldn't think of anything.

The old fly fisherman explained, "All fish, like most living things, require a certain habitat to thrive—even to survive." He looked at me to see if I seemed to understand him. I guess I must've looked like I did. "So," he continued, "to survive, trout are a type of fish that needs cold water that has a good amount of oxygen and little or no pollution, *and* a reliable food source. There are other things, but those are the basic ones."

I nodded and asked, "Can you tell me more?"

He glanced around and found a big boulder to sit on.

"I can, and I will." He waved his hand from left to right at the meandering creek. "Here, the water is slow-moving. It's exposed to the sun for long stretches because the woods were cleared generations ago for farming. The water heats up and is too warm for trout. Plus, there's less oxygen in it. Upstream, where the rapids and riffles are, some springs feed the creek, and the rapids oxygenate the water. Fast-moving water has more oxygen in it. In the springtime, when the entire creek has been cooled by run-off from the snowmelt, trout can comfortably swim anywhere they please, even along here. That's why a month ago, when we met, I caught a trout down here. By now, all the trout have returned to the rapids upstream or deep holes where cold springs feed the creek. That's where I'm heading."

Then he smiled, slapped his leg, and pushed himself up from the boulder. "Piece of advice?" he asked.

"Sure!"

"When you meet someone for the first time, look them in the eye and try to memorize their name. If they extend their hand, shake it firmly, like you mean it. You might not remember their name every time, but if you try, well, that's the point; you're giving them the respect they deserve."

I liked what he said, and took it to heart, but I felt ashamed, and when I gave him an awkward smile. I guess he could see my discomfort. I think he felt bad but shook it off.

"Good luck, Sam. Catching these chubs is still fun and good practice for catching other kinds of fish." Mr. Sands pointed into the clearing. "And another thing. Did you build these shelters?"

"Yes, sir."

"Fine job. Very fine job."

He started walking up the creek.

But how do I fly fish? I wanted to call after him to ask if he would teach me, but all I could think to say was, "Thank you for the lessons!"

Mr. Sands turned, smiled, winked, and waved before disappearing through the alders. I could hear him call back, "You got it, kiddo."

That evening, I again looked through the old Scout manual and some old Field & Stream magazines. The fishing articles were interesting, but I noticed they were mostly about bait fishing with spinning gear. I wanted to learn to flyfish. When Mother finally joined me shortly before bedtime, I again asked when I might get a lesson.

"I saw the old man again today, down at the creek."

She looked up at me. "Did you talk to him?"

I nodded. "His name is Mr. Sands."

"What did you talk about?"

"He told me what kind of water trout need to live," I replied, "and why this time of year I catch only chubs between the big maples." She looked like her mind was working on something.

"That's only the second time you've spoken to him?"

"Yes." I thought for a moment. "Do you know Mr. Sands?"

Mother shook her head. "No, but I know who he is. He's retired and a widower."

Widower, I thought. I didn't take long to figure it out. I knew what a widow was.

"He was a teacher," she continued, "and I've seen him walking here and there with his fly rod for years. He must love to fish. Your father used to see him with his rod and creel and say he was going to introduce himself and ask if he'd like some company on the river. Don't know if he ever did." She opened her book and switched on her reading lamp. "Let me know when you see him again. I'd like to speak to him."

"Okay." *I wonder what she wants with him. She probably wants to ask if I'm bothering him.*

Eight
A TASTE OF MIDDLE SCHOOL

At school, in Mrs. Cowan's sixth-grade class, the students were divided into small teams for projects to prepare for a bake sale.

"This will be fun," Mrs. Cowan said. "We need four signs announcing the bake sale, two for the fence out by the sidewalk where you all are dropped off and picked up, one for the town hall, and one for Freeze's Department store."

All the boys groaned—all except Sam, who sat motionless at his desk.

"Now, boys, no moaning. I want your best efforts. Some of the money we get from the sale will go toward buying some new basketballs and kickballs. Some of you have complained that most of them won't hold air."

The boys weren't happy about crafting poster board signs, but at least now they were invested.

Mrs. Cowan arranged the teams. Finally, she looked at Sam. "That leaves you three. Sam, you help Annie and Karen. Remember, everyone, the signs need to be colorful and with neat lettering. They should say only what needs to be said. 'Bake Sale.' That it's this Saturday at town hall and that it's to raise money for school supplies."

Sam breathed a quiet sigh of relief. It couldn't have gone better. Even though he had been held back in fifth grade and was a year older than the rest of the class, he knew if Mrs. Cowan had teamed him with any of the boys, they would have picked on him. Somehow, some way, they would've teased him. But Sam felt this team was the best scenario for him. Karen Hamm, who was a bossy perfectionist and tried to take over every school project, would surely do it now, and Annie Heath, the sweetest girl in class, would, in an effort to keep the peace, go along with whatever Karen said. All Sam would have to do would be to sit with them and pretend to look interested. Easy- peasy.

Karen Hamm laid out on the table a poster board, some colored markers and construction paper, two glue sticks, and some pencils into neat, organized piles. She rearranged them several times, not letting Annie touch anything. Sam sat resting his elbow on the table, his chin in his hand, looking focused and very interested in what Karen was doing. He was daydreaming about catching chubs down at the creek.

"First," Karen said, mostly to Annie, "we have to cut out some pictures of cookies and cupcakes. I'll draw the outlines on the colored paper, and you and Sam can cut them out. Then I'll color them and we'll glue them onto the poster."

Annie and Sam dutifully did as Karen said. Sam was good with scissors. As each cut-out was done, Karen took it and, with markers, drew frosting, sprinkles, or chocolate chips. Then, one at a time, she glued them onto the poster board. They were not placed willy-nilly; each cupcake was placed according to Karen's vision. Everything was perfect.

Mrs. Cowan walked amongst the class, inspecting the progress. "Now, I want everyone involved," she said as she hovered over Karen's poster.

Loud enough for Mrs. Cowan to hear, Karen said, "Sam, you write 'Bake Sale' along the top of the poster, just there—above where we've glued the cookies."

Sam was rocked. Everything had been going so well he had let his guard down! If he was paying attention, he could have acted when he saw Mrs. Cowan approaching their table. He could've asked her to go to the bathroom; or say his stomach hurt—anything to distract her! But he didn't. Now he had to do something. Now he had to try.

Sam thought quickly. In fact, his mind was racing. He couldn't figure any way to get out of it without it being too obvious. *Okay, 'Bake Sale.' That's pretty easy ... I can do this.*

Sam picked up a red marker. "Not red," Karen snapped, "use blue." He put down the red one and picked up a blue marker. He stared at the poster board.

"Here," Karen said. "Make the letters this tall." She made very light pencil marks, about three inches tall, where the letters should be."

"Can't you just do it?" Sam asked.

"You heard Mrs. Cowan. Besides, I have two more cupcakes to color in."

Sam focused hard on the board. He squinted. He grimaced. He shifted in his seat, and he carefully wrote, 'Bake Sale.' The letters were neat and quite symmetrical. Okay, he thought. That'll have to do.

Suddenly he jumped as Karen said. "Sam! You ruined it! You're so stupid. Now we have to start all over!" Karen said it plenty loud enough for everyone to hear, including Mrs. Cowan, who glided over to their table.

"Karen Hamm, we don't call other people stupid. You know better than that."

"I'm sorry, but Sam ruined our poster that we were almost done with."

Deanne Cowan was a good teacher, one of the best at Milton Middle School, but when Sam had been held back the year before and still showed little progress, she had been unsure how to handle his slower learning abilities. She was patient with him and gave him as much extra attention as she could, but there were thirteen other pupils in the class. She looked at the poster with the big blue letters, '**BACK SAEL**.'

Sam's head was down. He could hear Joey Higgins laughing at him. Sam panicked, jumped up, and said, "I have to go to the bathroom," and was already headed for the door before Mrs. Cowan, who felt terrible, could say, "All right."

"The rest of you, focus on your projects, please."

Minutes later, Annie Heath raised her hand and also asked to use the restroom. Annie walked down the empty hallway to the bathrooms. She turned the corner as Sam was coming out of the boy's room. He saw Annie and, lowering his eyes, shook his head. She stepped in front of him.

"I'm sorry Karen was so rude to you. My mom says, 'If you can't say something nice about someone, don't say anything at all.'"

Sam slid down the wall, sat on the floor, and drew his knees up to his chest. "I don't know what's wrong with me, I really don't. Except that I'm stupid."

Annie sat next to him. "Sam, you're not stupid at all. I think you're smart." Sam shook his head and sniffed.

"Do you know I have an uncle who couldn't read or write until he was in high school?" Sam looked up at Annie and shook his head again. "It's true," she said. "My dad said his brother—my uncle—had to have a special teacher who came to their house on the weekends for a year. You know what Uncle Ed does now? He runs the tower at the airport. He makes sure planes can take off and land safely. It's an important job. If he was stupid, planes would crash. People would die."

Annie put her arm around Sam. "Anyways, you're not stupid. *Karen* is. She just doesn't know it. I told her all we had to do was use some stenciled letters and glue them over the blue words. It only took a few seconds. It looks good."

Annie and Sam pushed themselves up from the floor. When they returned to the classroom, everything was back to normal. Sam slid into his chair. Mrs. Cowan walked up to his desk. "Are you okay, Sam?" He nodded.

"Karen?" Mrs. Cowan said.

Karen turned in her chair. "I'm sorry I yelled at you, Sam. We fixed the poster."

Mrs. Cowan glared over her glasses at Karen. "*And*, I'm sorry I called you stupid. No one in the class is stupid."

Sam flashed a look at Annie, and they both tried to keep from laughing.

Nine

Mr. Sands Comes to the Farm

Three weeks later, Rachel Candage was on her knees in one of the three greenhouses transplanting small roots of perennial plants from damp burlap bags into one-gallon plastic nursery pots. The pots were all filled with potting soil to about an inch from the top. Rachel pulled out a section of root, glanced at it to see which end of the root needed to point down into the dirt, and with the other hand, she poked a hole in the soil with three fingers. She then shoved the root into the dirt unceremoniously. She shook the pot to cover the root with soil and then shoved it aside, grabbed another, and repeated the process. It was something to watch her; some days, she could plant a hundred pots in about twenty-five minutes.

Sam, having finished all his chores for the day, was off exploring.

Rachel, in her transplanting trance, thought she heard something and sat back on her calves.

"Hello?" came a man's voice from the driveway.

"In here," she called, "house number two!" She rose to see who it was. She wasn't expecting any deliveries today, but sometimes plant seedlings, nursery supplies, or bags of potting soil arrived a day early or a day late. The greenhouse door swung open and in came the old man from the creek with a gentle smile on his face.

"Good morning," he said.

"Yes, good morning." Rachel replied. "Though it doesn't feel like morning now."

The old man looked around and breathed in deeply. Still smiling, he asked, "What time did you start?"

"A little before five o'clock."

"Almost five hours already," the man mumbled without looking at his watch. He extended his hand, and Rachel stepped forward to take it.

"Alton Sands."

"Rachel Candage. I'm afraid we're not open for another month…"

She knew who Mr. Sands was, and before he could respond, she continued, "Oh, yes—Mr. Sands!" She instantly had her suspicions as to why he was visiting. "Are you here about Sam? He mentioned he had met you. I hope he hasn't been pestering you."

"No, ma'am. Well, yes, I am here about Sam, but no—he hasn't been pestering me at all. He's quite a respectful young man."

Rachel waited for Mr. Sands to continue. He breathed in deeply again.

"I do love the smell of a greenhouse," he said.

"Most people seem to," Rachel replied. She wearily looked around at the neat rows of plastic pots. "Honestly, I don't really smell the soil and the sphagnum anymore. I used to love it, but after a few years, it begins to smell like work. The thing about the nursery business is, the sun, the clouds, the insects, fungi; everything seems out to get you."

Mr. Sands nodded. "To me, I guess it smells like springtime."

"Well, Mr. Sands, any time you need a little springtime, just come on in and smell away. But I'll warn you, if you stay awhile, I might put you to work."

"I wouldn't mind that," Mr. Sands replied. "And please, call me Alton. Or Al."

"All right," Rachel said. "I like the name Alton. So, what brings you by?"

"I suppose you've seen me cut through the lower fields on the way to the creek to fish?"

Rachel nodded.

"I do appreciate the access," he said. "It's getting harder to get to good fishing water these days. If I can get to the creek through your field, it's easier walking from there than through the woods to get upstream where the trout are."

Rachel bent down and picked up a sack of perennial roots. "You're welcome to anytime."

"Thank you. Those look like hostas."

Rachel glanced up at him, smiled, and nodded.

"And I have run into Sam a few times down by the creek," he continued.

"You're *sure* he hasn't pestered you?" Rachel asked again.

"No ma'am. But, he has seemed like he wanted someone to talk to … to interact with."

"What is up with this 'ma'am' thing?" Rachel said almost laughing.

Alton grinned. "Sorry—Rachel. Probably just my upbringing."

Rachel continued, "Yes, Sam does get lonely sometimes. There aren't any children around here even close to his age and for long periods of time, he only has me and my friend, Teri, to be around. He doesn't complain, but I know he gets starved for someone different to spend time with."

Rachel again looked around at the plant pots. In rows in front of her were hundreds of pots filled with soil awaiting seedlings. "The farm takes up so much of my time." She then turned her head toward the old man and looked him in the eyes.

"Alton, it's just Sam and me here on the farm, though Teri is here almost daily. I lost my husband in an accident some years ago. That's why Sam gets so lonely."

"Yes, Ma'am—*Rachel.* I was still teaching then, over in Dover. I remember the news." He bent his head down and then met her gaze again. "Communities all around were devastated. Your husband was well-liked."

She looked up at him again. "Did you meet him?"

"I did. I had the pleasure of meeting Jody several times."

Rachel went back to work, shoving roots down into the soft soil. "People were so good to us when it happened. They sent food, money, cards, and letters. Someone even anonymously sent a beautiful watercolor of my husband fly fishing. In it, Jody is standing out on the Ledges Pool on the river, casting in the evening light. The painting is unsigned, but there was a small note with it that just said, "*So sorry for your loss—it is everyone's loss.*" That 11" x 8" piece of art has become one of my prized possessions."

Alton breathed deeply for the third time, smelling the sweet aroma from the potting soil. Then he changed the subject. "Well, I really stopped by for two reasons. As I said, I wanted to thank you for letting me pass through your property to the creek, and secondly, I'd like to offer to teach Sam how to flyfish. *If* you think it's a good idea, that is."

Rachel stopped planting. Alton had a kind face. His smile was as sincere as a smile can get. In fact, he exuded kindness and gentleness. "I know you were a teacher, Alton. What subjects did you teach?"

"English and Biology."

"Did you have any children of your own?"

"My wife and I were never blessed, I'm sad to say. And she passed away some years ago. But, I had my students." Alton smiled again.

Rachel stood and again outstretched her hand. Alton grasped it.

"Well, Mr. Alton Sands," Rachel said, winking, "You're hired."

"Great. What would be the best day and time to start?"

"I try not to give him too many farm chores so that he's usually done by mid-morning. I want him to have time to play—and to fish."

"Tomorrow at eleven, then. We can start with casting lessons here, on the lawn. That way, he won't be distracted by the stream and daydreams of catching big fish."

"Understood," Rachel said. "I'll get out Jody's old rod and reel. But the line will be old."

"No need. He probably shouldn't learn on an expensive bamboo rod. I collected rods for years. I'll pick out an old fly rod and reel he can have. My pleasure."

With that, Alton Sands walked back up the driveway. He hadn't driven, though he lived miles away. He was known to drive a beautiful old Willys Jeep, but he seemed to walk everywhere.

As she watched him walk out onto the main road, Rachel thought, *I can't imagine Sam hasn't been pestering the poor man. He even must have told him about his dad's old bamboo rods.*

⁂

I was sitting on the rock wall that lines the edge of the woods, resting after finishing my chores and watching for the red-tailed hawk that hunts our crop fields every day. Sometimes she circles far up in the sky, so far it seems impossible she could see a mouse on the ground from there, and sometimes she cruises the field only inches from the soil. I've seen her catch mice before. She's very fast. I occasionally see her catch a mourning dove or a pigeon, which she takes to the top of a tree or one of our utility poles and pulls all the feathers out of the carcass before she eats it.

A movement caught my eye, and I saw Mr. Sands walking along the road without his fishing pole. I gave a bird whistle, and he looked in my direction and waved. I waved back but stayed put. *He must just be out for a walk*, I thought. I wanted to talk to him, but Mother told me not to bother him.

I had fished for a couple of hours and had caught a few chubs until I ran out of worms. I wasn't in the mood to go up behind the barn and dig for more in the ancient manure piles that now were grassy mounds. Those mounds held thousands of angle worms. For a moment, I contemplated going outside after dark with a flashlight to catch some nightcrawlers, which I did occasionally, but I hated how slimy they felt. Afterward, I couldn't wash my hands long or hard enough.

The fields were ablaze with patches of daisies, buttercup, and my favorite, the fiery orange hawkweed. Teri knew all the names of the wildflowers and liked to teach them to me.

I walked back to the creek to get the red wagon and my fishing pole. As I strode up to the streambank, a large dragonfly buzzed along the water's surface. As often happened, I became fascinated by the flowing water in the little creek. It was beautiful, certainly, but what fascinated me was the amount of life along its banks. Every square foot of the streambank seemed to hold life. I lay down on my belly and studied closely. I could see dozens of microworlds — or thought I could. The motionless frog, the water bugs skittering on the water's surface, and the tiny insects that moved along the underwater sand and gravel.

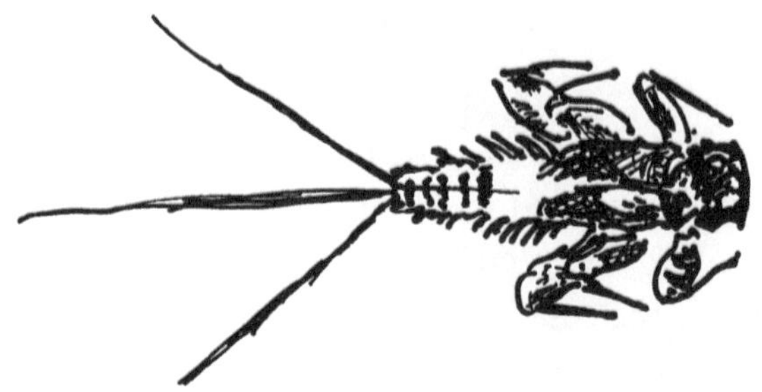

The underwater bugs didn't look like regular insects at all, and I had to stare at one spot of stream bottom for quite a while before I could see them. Even the plants along the banks interested me. The plants in Mom's greenhouses held no particular fascination for me, but the wild ones did. There were so many wild, curious things living along the creek that I was constantly reminded of how very little I knew about nature. The one thing I did know was that I wanted to learn more about it.

Before I knew it, hours had passed. With the afternoon shadows slanting through the trees, I picked up the fishing rod and wagon handle and headed for home. I hadn't even fished; the insects had stolen the day.

Tomorrow I would explore some more.

Ten

THE LESSONS BEGIN

At supper, Mother broke the news; Mr. Sands had stopped by to talk to her.

Oh, crap, I've done something wrong, I thought. I didn't think I had bothered him that much. I sat still, trying hard not to slurp my soup, ready to take my lecture.

"I'm always so proud of you, Sam," she said.

Oh, no...I've really messed up if she's starting with that. What on earth have I done?

She continued, "Not many other kids your age have to help their parents with their jobs, but you do, and yet you never complain. Plus, you put in a lot of time to get your homework done—even though it's hard, and though I know you would rather be outside exploring or fishing, you try so hard to work on your reading. The trying hard ... that's the important thing. Your dad would have loved all those things about you."

"Have I ... messed up, Mom?"

"What?! Lord, no," she smiled at me. "Mr. Sands came by to ask permission to teach you to fly fish."

I almost choked on my soup. "He did? Oh, that's great."

"Yes. He's a lovely man. I think it would be a good thing."

I sat back in my chair and stared at my food. I smiled at her and went back to eating. Almost a minute passed before I spoke again. "Did he say when?"

"Tomorrow. He's coming here to the farm."

"Not the creek?"

Mother shook her head and swallowed a bite of chicken before answering. "No, he said the first few lessons will be how to cast a fly rod. He's going to teach you here, on the lawn."

I nodded. "You should see him fish, Mom. It's really something to see him cast. It's pretty."

In the morning, I got up extra early to be sure my chores were done before 11:00. There were over 400 hanging baskets filled with combinations of colorful flowers, and I had to water each one with a four-foot-long wand that was attached to a garden hose. With the water running continuously out of the end of the wand, I would walk down every row in each greenhouse with the long wand, dragging the hose behind me. I needed to pay close attention and water them all. If later in the day the sun came out, any basket I missed would die, simple as that. I hooked the angled spout of the wand into each basket and counted to four. That was usually enough water to hold them until the afternoon. One day a year earlier, when I had just started taking on the morning watering duties, I missed an entire row of hanging baskets. By noon they were all dead as could be.

"Samuel!" Mom was furious at me. "You have to pay attention! This row of baskets would've paid for a month's worth of heating oil, of for your next year's school clothes! Just—go." I cried and spent the rest of the day in my room. I thought seriously about running away, so that I couldn't make a mistake like that ever again. Then, later that night, Mom cried when she talked to me about it.

"I'm sorry I yelled so hard, Sam. It's not your fault. You're only eleven. I wish I didn't have to ask you to take on such responsibility at your age, but I'm stuck between a rock and a hard place—I can't afford to hire any help, but I have to fill the greenhouses to make them profitable. I apologize."

I gave her a big hug. "But I want to help you."

That was when she cried.

After watering the plants, my only other chore was to carry plastic pots filled with soil from one greenhouse into another, where Mother would later transplant small seedlings into them. On this morning, I'd guess there were probably 250 pots, and by sticking my thumb into the rim of one pot and my fingers into another, I could carry two in each hand. It was over 60 trips from one house to the next one, but by not stopping it only took an hour.

I got cleaned up and was ready for my lesson by ten o'clock. While I waited, I found a few old magazine articles about fly fishing. Outside, on the big, covered porch, sitting in one of the rocking chairs that overlooked the driveway, I looked at the photos in the articles. I waited for Mr. Sands to arrive. I was pretty excited to learn.

At quarter till eleven, a very old, green Jeep rolled down the driveway. It had a red canoe tied to the roof, and a spare tire bolted to the top of the hood. Mr. Sands smiled and waved through the windshield as he pulled up to the farmhouse. He parked off to the side and got out.

"Morning, Sam."

"Good morning, Mr. Sands," I replied. I would never forget his name again.

Mr. Sands stepped to the back of the Jeep and removed a canvas bag and two metal tubes. He carried them to the porch steps and sat on the top tread.

Mother had heard the Jeep and stepped out of greenhouse Number 3. "Hi, Alton."

"Morning," he replied. "We're just about to get started."

"Great. Sam has been raring to go all morning. How long do you think you'll need for the first lesson, Al?"

"About an hour, maybe a little more. I don't want to overwhelm him with information on the first day, or he might forget some of the fundamentals before he gets going." Mr. Sands winked at me as he said that. I tried to wink back, but I've never been able to wink, and ended up blinking at him.

"Perfect," said Mother. "I'll have lunch ready for you both around twelve-thirty."

Mr. Sands nodded at her. "C'mon, Sam. Let's get started." I followed him to the lawn by the barn. As we walked, he said, “You know, there will be much to learn about the cast, the equipment, and about the fish. But, before we fish, you’ll need to learn how to cast—at least a little. If we were to jump right in streamside and you started flailing the fly rod, you’d get tangled a lot, frustrated, and maybe get soured on the thing. It’ll be best if we have a couple of lessons right here in the yard. If you practice a little, you’ll be catching fish with flies in short order.”

“Whatever you think, sir,” I said. “I learn pretty fast from listening. That’s what Teri always says about me, anyhow.”

Mr. Sands laid his equipment on the grass and turned to me. “I know I’m probably older than your grandparents, but unless your mother says differently, I think you should just call me Alton. It’s easier on the ears.”

“Yes, sir – *Alton.*”

He smiled at me and pulled three sections of a rod from one of the tubes. He handed them to me and removed the second rod.

“First, an anatomy lesson. Do you know what anatomy is?”

“The human body?”

“Well, yes, its parts, anyway. Anatomy is from the Greek word for dissection—cutting open something to study its parts. It’s a word that’s supposed to be used for the study of living organisms, but I think it’s a good word for the parts of a fly rod because when you’re standing in a stream fishing and the conditions are just right, and there’s an insect hatch, and you’re being enveloped by the beautiful nature all around you, the rod becomes more than an instrument. It becomes an extension of your brain and your arm, and when everything comes together perfectly, you, the rod, and the fly line sort of become parts of a living thing, and part of the river.”

Alton looked at me as if he was teasing, but I could tell he meant what he said. I didn’t know how to respond to that.

“You’ll see what I mean someday,” he said. “So, Sam, this is the anatomy of the fly rod: the cork handle, or grip, is obvious. Built into the handle is the reel seat — also obvious. I’ll show you how to mount the reel in a minute. Farther up the rod from the handle is the first ‘guide,’ similar to the ones on your spinning rod, where the line will pass through. This first guide is called the ‘stripping guide’ and is typically built a little differently than all the others." Then, he pointed to the sections of the rod. "I've noticed your spinning rod is a one-piece, but these rods are usually two-pieces or sometimes more."

He pointed to the ends of one of the rod sections. "This short metal tube—the female end—and a matching metal cap, the male end, are built into the end of each rod section. They're called ferrules, and they connect the rod's sections together. Now, before putting them together, the old-timers used to wipe the male ends of the ferrules with their fingers, and they'd pass them through their hair to pick up some of the natural oils that are usually present there. They said it made separating the ferrules easier, but I'm not sure if that works. Does help to keep them clean, though."

Alton showed me the rest of the guides, each one getting smaller as they got closer to the tip of the rod. He showed me how to line the guides up and gently slide each rod section into the next ferrule until I held in my hand a wispy nine-foot flyrod. Then, he showed me how to seat the reel and secure it with the thumbscrew. The rod felt a lot different in my hand than my spinning rod did. I was about to find out how different they were.

Once the reel was secured in its seat, Alton pulled about fifteen feet of fly line off the spool. There was a clear section of line attached to the thicker, light brown fly line. He called the clear section the "leader." I watched intently as the old teacher folded a few inches of the end of the fly line upon itself to make a sort of loop, and started feeding the loop through each guide, the leader trailing behind. When he got near the smallest guide at the far tip of the rod, he said, "Watch this..." and let go of the fly line. Instead of all the line snaking back down through the guides and onto the ground, the loop tried to unfold and was stuck in the small metal guide and stayed put.

"Saves you the trouble of having to start re-stringing it over again if you accidentally let go of the line, which can be maddening when you're trying to rig up a rod, and the trout are jumping everywhere."

I nodded.

Alton re-grabbed the loop, pulled it through the final guide, and then pulled the leader all the way through. The rod was rigged and ready.

"There you go," Alton said, handing me the rod again. Now the rod felt different. The weight of the line strung through the guides made the rod feel more balanced. I liked the feel of it in my hand.

"Check to make sure you didn't miss any guides before moving on; nothing is more frustrating than rigging up the rod with your favorite fly, and then it won't cast properly, only to find out you missed a guide."

I checked. I hadn't missed any.

"Move it around a bit," Alton suggested. "Waggle it. Get a feel for it and tell me what you think."

When I waggled it, the flexible tip flicked back and forth, and the five or six feet of fly line and the leader responded and flipped around in the air. I had the sensation that with my hand around that thin cork handle, I had complete control of the line. I liked the feel of the outfit in my hand very much. It was new and exciting.

"Well?" Alton asked.

I looked up at him, lost for words.

"What do you think? Or feel?" he asked.

I shook my head a single time. "I fish an awful lot," I said. "I guess what I feel is everything is different now."

Alton straightened up and grinned at me again. He looked surprised at my answer. He removed his old, battered, brimmed fishing hat and wiped his forehead with his shirt sleeve. Then he simply nodded.

He was still smiling as he peered across the bottom field in the direction of the creek. I couldn't understand why he suddenly looked sad. Maybe not sad, but as if his mind was somewhere else.

"All right," he blurted out. "And now we learn to cast."

Alton positioned us so there was plenty of room behind and in front of us. "It's best, if possible," he said, "to learn to cast on the water. And we will. But today, we're going over the gear and a few fundamentals. Whatever day next that your mom says we can proceed, I know a good spot down the creek a little way where we can really get some casting done."

"It's a lot to learn," I said, "but I can't wait."

Alton glanced at me again. He seemed to get a kick out of things I said, but I didn't know why.

Eleven

I Get Rhythm

We walked farther out onto the mowed lawn beside the barn where there would be even more room. He stood next to me, each of us holding a fly rod.

"Most people think months of practice are needed before one can be a good fly caster," he said, "but they're wrong. The truth is that fly-casting is not very difficult. Not if you have some basic instruction at the beginning. It can be learned by anyone who is willing to follow those few instructions. Then the newbie will be able to get the fly onto the water and catch fish, but, as with anything in life, practice forms the background of any skill. If you want to master the sport of flyfishing, you'll have to practice over time. It doesn't matter if you want to get very good at flyfishing or simply good enough to catch fish — it's up to you. You shouldn't worry about that yet."

I nodded at him. He pulled some line from his reel and twitched the tip of the rod, sending the line through the guides and out onto the grass.

"Sometimes," Alton said, "the beginner will want to see how far he or she can throw their line. This isn't necessary. What's more important than distance is *where* you cast, and how well you present your fly to the fish. It's all about accuracy. So, in the beginning, it will be best if you concentrate on getting proficient at making short, accurate casts of maybe twenty-five feet. Make sense?"

Again, I nodded. I was used to filling in the blanks when I didn't know what a word meant. I guessed that 'proficient' meant 'good.'

"Let's start with the fly line," he offered. "In bait casting with a spinning rod like the one you've been using, the fisherman depends upon the weight of the lure, in addition to the action of the rod, to pull their line off the reel during the cast. When fly casting, it's just the opposite; the weight of the line, propelled through the air by *your* casting technique and the action of the rod, pulls the lure behind it. It's not the fly you cast, it's the line itself. You with me so far?"

"Yes, sir. I cast the line; the line pulls the fly through the air."

"You got it. That means, before we cast, we need to let out some line. It's called 'paying out line.' It won't come off the reel by itself." The teacher paused for a moment and said, "In fact, I think the line is most important … it's the heart of a good cast. The line works together with the action of the rod *and* how well the caster uses the rod." He studied me for a moment and then said, "They all work together."

Mr. Sands pulled more line off his reel, one arms-length at a time, to demonstrate. From the tip of the rod he pulled seven or eight feet of line with the leader attached. The rest of the line he had stripped from the reel was in a small pile on the ground at his feet.

"Now," Mr. Sands began, "before we cast, we need to find a grip that's comfortable for you. There are several ways to grip a flyrod, but I think you should start with the most common one used."

I watched how he gripped the cork handle of his rod and copied it. He held the rod in his right hand with his thumb extended along the back of the cork grip opposite the reel. The four fingers just wrapped around and gripped the cork. Easy. I did the same with my rod, and Mr. Sands—*Alton* (that was going to take some getting used to) wrapped his huge hand around mine and repositioned it slightly, then let go.

"There," he said, "how's that feel?"

"Great!"

"Good. Now remember that grip, and how it feels. If it always feels natural and comfortable, there's no need to ever change it."

I looked at my hand and tilted the rod handle this-way-and-that and committed the grip to memory.

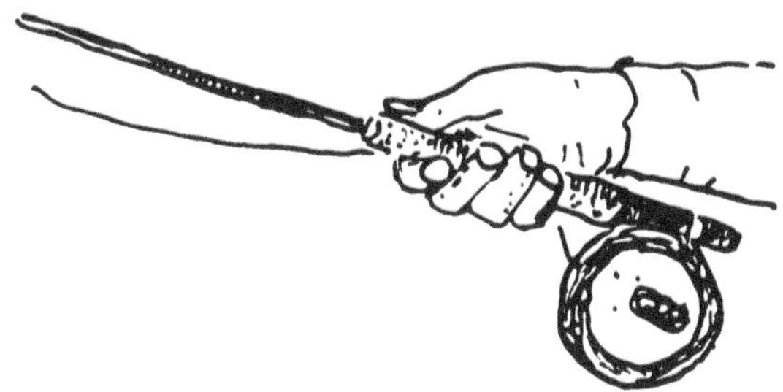

"There are many variations of a forward cast," said Alton, "but today, we're going to focus on just two. The roll cast and the basic forward cast. If you can get those two down with some proficiency, you'll be able to fish the creek *and* the river.

"The roll cast is important to learn because most of your fishing for a while at least will be at the creek, which, because of the trees and bushes, often doesn't have much room for a backcast. It's not a pretty cast for the newbie, but when an angler gets good at roll casting, it's lovely indeed."

I nodded to let him know I understood. There was that word 'proficiency' again; I made a mental note to ask Mom about it later.

"The roll cast," Alton said, "permits you to get out a fair amount of line with a minimum amount of space behind you — once you get a good bit of line off the reel and out through the guides." He demonstrated, and I copied him.

He watched me as I did it. With each arm's length of fly line I pulled off the reel, I would point the rod tip downward and waggle it until on the lawn in front of me was about twenty feet of line in a pile. Then, using his rod, he showed me what to do.

Alton lifted his rod straight up over his head. Some of the line dragged on the ground toward him, then he gently snapped the rod forward, almost parallel to the lawn. The line rose off the ground and shot out through the guides, laying itself out into a straight line on the grass.

Now was my turn. I pictured what he had just done, and in my mind, I broke it down into three parts: the raising of the rod high overhead, watching for the loop to form toward me, and the dropping of the rod tip. I hesitated and then did it. It wasn't as smooth as when Alton had done it, but it worked. The line did shoot out the guides, and it laid out straight. I looked at it. My first try, and it was definitely far enough to catch a fish.

"Oh, man ..." I said.

Alton had me do it a few more times, adjusting this and that so I was consistent.

"In most other casts, I'll teach you to keep your casting elbow tucked close to your side, letting the rod do most of the work. But with a roll cast, before you forward cast, if you raise your arm up overhead and extend the rod skyward, it'll help."

I tried that, and the line shot out farther.

"It's physics," he continued. "By raising the rod up higher, you're increasing the arc. You can learn about physics when you get to high school if you choose to."

All I knew was I could now do a roll cast.

"All right," he said. "Practice that whenever you get the chance. Now, we'll tackle the basic forward fly cast.

"We already have the line out; pretend it's on the water. The first part of a cast is called the 'haul,' which some teachers call the 'pick-up.' Just before you start the backcast, reach up with your left hand near the first guide and grasp the fly line. Then pull it toward yourself, next to your left thigh. As you do, lift the rod sharply upright with enough force to propel the line its full length behind you. You don't want the rod tip to go farther back than here ..." Alton held the rod straight up above his head. "The problems most beginners have are they take the rod too far back while casting, or they let their wrist bend. Both mistakes will ruin the cast."

Alton said, "Here ..." He took my hand holding the rod and, holding my wrist rigid, lifted the rod upright, straight up to the sky. "Right here," he continued, "try not to go farther back than here. That's called the 'twelve o'clock' position, with the rod pointing straight up overhead. If you happen to go just a bit too far back, say to the 'two o'clock position, you'll still be all right."

He demonstrated the rod positions several times. "Here's twelve o'clock," he said, and, moving the backcast a little farther behind us, "two o'clock. Understand?"

"Yes, I think so." It seemed simple enough.

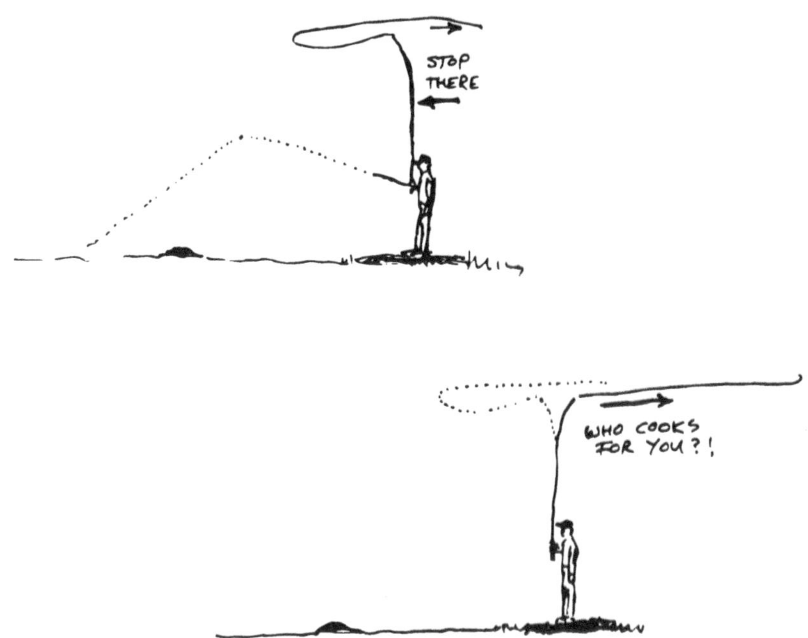

"These few things," Alton reiterated, "especially the rod positions; keeping the elbow tucked to your side, I call it keeping the elbow 'quiet,' and keeping the wrist rigid are the keys for a beginner. You work on these things, and you'll be a flyfisher in no time. Whenever it feels wrong, slow down the entire cast. You'll get the rhythm.

"Now, let's give it a try."

I thought for a moment, then brought the rod up to the twelve o'clock position and quickly back down again. The line fell into a pile at my feet.

"That's fine," Alton said, "but the whole thing is much slower.

I tried again, but it wasn't much better.

"Here," he said, "like this." Alton demonstrated some beautiful, graceful casts. "Before you try again, do you know the sound that the barred owl makes at the edge of the field when the sun goes down?"

I nodded. "It's always four," I said. "Who, who, who-who."

"Yes," Alton replied. "My wife used to say it sounded like the owl was calling out, '*Who cooks for you*?'"

I smiled up at him. "Yeah, they do sound like that."

"All right, how about when you make your backcast and get your rod tip up to between the twelve o'clock and two o'clock positions, you say aloud, "*Who cooks for you?*" then start your down with your forward cast. That should put your timing just about right."

"Okay," I said. I thought for a moment, focusing, and then did just what he suggested.

That was it! The line shot through the guides and laid out on the lawn in a nice, straight cast. I was thrilled, and so was Alton.

"There you go!" he said. "That's all there is to it. That's the timing you'll need."

I made a dozen more casts using the owl's *who cooks for you* call, and the casts got better each time. Alton said I was a natural, patted me on the back, and strangely I felt like I was going to be able to do it. In fact, I felt at that moment that I could do almost anything—not a common feeling for me.

"I think that'll be enough for you to think of and practice for now," said my teacher. "There's much, much more you can learn about fly fishing if you choose to, but you have a lot of time. Work on these things whenever you get the time, and next week we'll see how your form looks and go from there. Then, we'll get you on the water."

"Yes, sir," I replied. I was waggling the tip of the rod again. I liked the feel of it in my hand.

"Will you be okay practicing casting for a few days?" he asked. "I remember when I was your age, I wanted to be down at the pond fishing all the time."

"Yes," I replied. "I can practice. Mom says I have a lot of patience for a boy my age. She says the farm has taught me that. To tell the truth, I'm not sure what she means."

The old man smiled again. "I have an idea what she means, and I bet she's correct."

"Mr. Sands?"

"Alton—unless you're too uncomfortable calling me that."

I shook my head. "Alton, in between my chores and practicing, can I still go to the creek with my spinning rod if I feel like fishing?"

The guy smiled at me an awful lot which made me feel like I said something dumb or had mispronounced a word. He bent closer and patted my shoulder. "Of course!" he said, almost laughing. "Fishing isn't about what technique you choose to use, it's more about being out there; in the woods and on the water, wishing for the time you could be there every minute of the day. Listening to the birds, catching glimpses of animals in the wild, and trying to fool the fish who are wary. As you get older, fishing helps you temporarily forget life's troubles. I swear, sometimes flyfishing can be like medicine." Alton stood back up, still smiling. "Medicine that doesn't taste bad. So, yes, fish as much with your spinning rod, as much as your chores and fly casting practice allows."

He showed me how to break down the rods and put them away. Then he handed me back the rod and reel I had been learning with. "But you'll need these to practice with," he said. "I want you to have these."

"For keeps?" I asked. Then I wondered if it would be okay with Mom.

"Yes, for keeps. If you take good care of this rod and reel, they'll take good care of you and help you through troubling times in your life. The line you'll have to replace every few years."

"Th … thank you." I wasn't sure what to say, *and* I had visions of Mother making me give it back.

"Now," Alton said, "let's see what your mom has made for lunch."

We both walked toward the house. "She's a heck of a cook," I said.

Alton laughed a little.

"But Teri's an even better cook. Have you met Teri yet?"

"No, I haven't."

"Oh, you'll love her. She's a part of the farm too."

We leaned our rod tubes against the side of the house, kicked off our shoes in the mudroom, and went into the kitchen.

Twelve

SECRETS & SCANDALMONGERS

By the time the end of May rolled around, we were having a good year. Mother's Day and Memorial Day, two big revenue-generating weekends for us had been our biggest flower-selling events so far. Mother made enough money from Memorial Day weekend alone to buy a new furnace for greenhouse No. 1. And I had been right about Al and Teri. When they met, they liked each other straight away.

As the end of my school year neared and I began getting more excited for a summer of fishing, a dark cloud came over the farm, a story I would not learn about for many years, of which I am grateful.

One Sunday afternoon while I was down at the creek fishing, Mom came home from grocery shopping and she was walking fast and her face was beet red. By the time I had returned and made my way onto the porch to read, she had collected herself but I could tell something was bothering her. When I asked if she was okay, she said she had a headache.

The next afternoon, while I was at school, Teri floated into the kitchen to have a cup of coffee with Mom.

She took one look at Mother and exclaimed, "Rachel, what's wrong?!"

"Oh, it's nothing. You know small towns … gossip tongues wag."

"What did you hear?"

"I don't want you getting angry and making a scene."

Teri was getting riled up, and good. "This town! Just tell me, does it involve you, Sam, me, or Alton?"

Mother looked at Teri but didn't answer. She did not have to. Teri finally sat in a chair. Her hand slapped down on the table. "You tell me what you heard."

Mother shook her head. "It's absurd. And grotesque in its implications. I have felt like throwing up since I heard it."

Teri was mad, and she knew it wasn't helping. So, she drew a deep breath, calmed herself, and said, "Look, maybe it's not so bad. Just tell me what you heard and we'll talk about it."

Mother did not want to tell her, but she also knew there was no way around it. "I'm telling you, it's crazy and horrible." She sighed and finally said, "I was at the grocery store yesterday, and from the next aisle I could hear that old biddy Marjorie Bart gossiping as usual. Normally, I don't care because I can't imagine anyone ever listens to her. But what she said this time shocked me to my core."

"Well, you're right about nobody caring about what Marjorie Bart says."

Mother looked at Teri. She paused and said, "I heard her say Alton's name. I listened closer, and Bart said, 'I just wonder about that old Alton Sands spending so much time in those woods with that Candage boy."

"What?!"

Mother nodded. The old gossiper said, "Mr. Sands lives alone. He's no kin to them. I just hope the mother knows what's going on. I hope there's nothing inappropriate."

Teri stood up, folding her arms in front of her. "You can't be serious! What was she implying?" Then she bent down and hugged mother.

"I don't know, exactly. And I know I shouldn't care what she thinks, but this is how rumors get started. You remember that nice young teacher up in Fort Smith? Some teenage girl seeking attention started spreading a rumor that he had touched her. He was suspended, they had an investigation, and he got fired. A few days later, the girl's father suspected his daughter was lying and he confronted her. She confessed to the principal, but the damage was done. The teacher knew he could never work in that small school system again and left town. Even though he was exonerated in all his paperwork, he couldn't find another teaching job. I felt so bad for that guy."

"At this point," Mother continued, "Bart hasn't accused Al of anything specific. But I feel I should confront her because if she continues out of boredom or an attempt to draw attention to herself, she could ruin him. And what if it does become a full-blown rumor? How would Sam handle it? God, Almighty—I don't even want to think about that."

Teri sat down. She leaned forward and in a calm voice said, "Rachel, I don't ever ask you for anything, do I?"

"No."

"We care about each other, all of us, right?"

"Yes. Very much."

"And you know how I feel about Sam and Alton?"

"Of course."

"Then I'm going to ask you now to let me handle this, and I'm going to ask you to trust me."

Mother knew Teri is as honest as a human can get. "You won't make things worse?"

Teri sat back in her chair. "I might, but I'm going try very hard not to. I will try to appeal to her and her gossiping cronies."

Mother nodded.

Teri was wound pretty tight as she drove around Milton the next morning. About noon, she finally spotted Marjorie Bart's car, parked in front of the only busy hair salon in town.

Teri parked across the street, got out, and marched toward the beauty solon steps, placing her red hair in a ponytail as she walked. She cleared all four steps in two strides and entered the salon. There was Marjorie sitting to her right, her hair wrapped in some sort of plastic wrap. There were four other patrons and two hair stylists. Willy McCutcheon, the owner-stylist, was in the rear of the salon mixing some chemicals.

"May I help you?" he called out.

"Nope," Teri said. "I'm here to help her." Teri stopped in front of Marjorie and pointed at her. Mrs. Bart recoiled. "Now," Teri began, first addressing all the patrons. "I know the gossip that goes on in hair salons, bars, and other places of business. It's completely wrong, but it has always happened and probably always will."

Teri looked at Bart. "Marjorie, we don't know each other well, but at least in a minute, we'll understand each other."

Mrs. Bart opened her slack jaw to speak back, but Teri put her hand up and said, "No!" Bart recoiled again and no sound came out. Teri quickly continued. "Yesterday at the grocery store, someone overheard you say something off-color about the wonderful Alton Sands." Marjorie looked down at her hands. "Now, so far, Marjorie, no harm has been done, not as far as I know." Teri addressed the room. "We're all part of a small community. A great community. But Marjorie, regardless if you're bored, unhappy, or self-righteous, whatever it is that makes people gossip and spread rumors, you need to know that rumors can steal people's reputations. They can do untold damage."

Marjorie Bart considered herself, with no evidence, to be superior to everyone in the room, and was chomping at the bit to retaliate and tell off Teri, but Teri did not give her the opportunity.

Before Bart could take a breath and speak, Teri continued. "I'm going to give you something, Marjorie, and then ask something from you in return. Even though it's none of your business, I'm going to explain Alton's, Sam's, Rachel's, and my relationship. Alton Sands, that jewel of a man whom everybody loves, has spent the last year volunteering to tutor Sam in a subject he has struggled with, and he has taught a fatherless boy how to fly fish. Through these lessons, Al has taught Sam about conservation, stewardship of the land, entomology, and stream biology.

He has taught the boy about construction. He has taught Sam many things about life. And I can tell you that Rachel and Sam consider Al to be one of their greatest gifts. If we could all be a bit more like Alton Sands, this would be a beautiful world. But instead, there are rumor-making scandalmongers who for some reason like to suck the beauty out of life. That's not us, is it, ladies?"

No one spoke. Teri's eyes were still fiery, and the room still felt very tense.

Teri looked Marjorie Bart in the eyes. "You go to church every Sunday, Marjorie." Teri pointed individually at the other patrons. "And so do you, and you, and you. So here's what I'm asking of you, Mrs. Bart. When you go home today, I want you to get out your Bible and re-read Exodus. Words matter to God, Marjorie, because they can harm as well as heal. When we bear false witness against our neighbors, we are breaking His commandment."

Teri leaned down close to Marjorie and in a whisper that only she could hear said, "You're going to reach out to the person you were talking to yesterday and tell her that you misspoke and that you've learned that Alton has once again helped others in the community. Understand?"

Marjorie didn't answer, but Teri knew she had gone as far as she could.

Teri turned and started to leave. "Thank you, ladies…and Willy." As she walked out the door, without looking back, she said, "Remember your assignment, everyone —Exodus."

Teri drove to the farm, found Rachel cleaning greenhouse No. 2, and started helping her. A full minute went by.

"Well?" Rachel asked.

"I found her getting her hair colored. Stormed in there and told her if she said another word about Alton, I would find her and she wouldn't have any hair left to color."

"You did not…"

"No, but that would've been fun." Teri winked at Mother. "I think we're good."

Teri was right as rain. Neither Alton nor I ever heard anything unsavory in the community, and no rumors seemed to circulate. A year later, the Elks Club in Milton gave Alton, who was not an Elk, a plaque for community service which made him very confused.

But Karma has her darlings. The hair stylist Willy McCutcheon was so distracted by Teri's confrontation at the salon he completely lost track of the developer and tint mixture, and Marjorie Bart's hair that day came out a rather shocking color of green. Willy could not correct it for fear the bleach would destroy what little hair she had left. She had no choice but to cover her head at all times, even in her own home. The green hair took over two months to fade away to the point that he could fix it, but by then it was too late.

Marjorie Bart was forever known to all the Milton kids as "the kerchief lady."

Thirteen

I Practice

Mom had made grilled cheese sandwiches and chicken soup for lunch, but her grilled cheese sandwiches were special. She baked the bread herself every Sunday. She added thin slices of tomatoes which came from greenhouse No. 3. In fact, I had planted the tomato seedlings myself. And Mom always spread the slightest smear of mustard (which Teri made) on one slice of the bread. Alton kept looking at the triangles of his sandwich as he ate them.

"This is the best grilled cheese I've ever had," he said. He was almost talking to himself. "And the soup is homemade. Incredible."

"Many thanks," Mother said.

After a pause, he added, "I just want to say, Sam is a great student."

Mom winked at me. "Well, that's nice to hear. We've noticed for a long time that he loves to learn about almost anything. It sort of comes naturally to him when he's given instruction. I really appreciate you teaching him to fly fish." She teasingly messed up my hair. "I wish his grades were a little better." Then she winked at me. "But they're good enough."

I just sat and ate my sandwich, wondering how this was going to play out.

"There will be a series of lessons if we do this right," Alton offered. "Sam's going to practice the basic things we went over today, and I'll come back next Wednesday, and we'll proceed. If that's okay, of course."

"Absolutely," Mom said. "And thank you for coming. It means a lot."

"May I have a piece of paper and a pencil?" Alton asked.

Mom got up and got both from the kitchen junk drawer. "Is this big enough paper?"

"Perfect." Alton began sketching something on the envelope-sized piece of paper. In only a minute, he slid the paper in front of me.

"This is to remind you how far back you can go with your backcast."

I looked at it. At first glance, it seemed like a stick figure of a man casting a fly rod with some writing under it, but when I looked closer, there was some detail in the drawing. For drawing it so quickly, the proportions were all correct, and it looked, I don't know … lifelike, I guess.

Mom looked at it. "Alton, you're an artist!"

"You're too kind," he said. "Dabbling in art has become one of my hobbies that I've embraced since my wife passed. But no, not a real artist."

After lunch and after offering to wash the dishes, Alton left. But, as he got into his old Jeep, he asked me, "Remember the four things?"

"I think so … not too far back, wrist straight, elbow 'quiet' (he smiled at that), and …"

Alton broke in and reminded me, "If it feels or looks wrong or awkward, just slow the cast down a bit—both forward and back. And remember to break down the rod and put it back into its tube whenever you're not using it."

"Yes. I will." And with a wink, he slid into the Jeep, called back, "*Who cooks for you?*" and was off.

Over the next week, I practiced every day. I looked at Alton's drawing of the man in the middle of the backcast, and it helped. The things we covered in the lesson were written below the drawing, and he was right. Whenever I tried to cast the line, and it either made a snapping noise in the air behind me or balled up in a pile in front of my feet, I would slow everything down, and it cast much better. I did take my spinning rod and reel to the creek a few times, but my heart wasn't in it as in the past. I caught a few chubs, and it was fun, but I felt like it was taking time away from my fly rod practicing.

When I told Mother that, she said, "Maybe that's because fly fishing has been in your blood all along and Alton is bringing it out."

I didn't know what she meant by that, but I knew I was excited to fly fish, and I knew I wanted to get as good as Alton someday.

When Wednesday finally arrived, I finished watering the plants early and was sitting on the porch waiting as Alton drove up the driveway. He instinctively parked in a spot where the old Jeep would be out of the way of the tractor or any cars that may want to get by.

"Morning," he said, carrying his vest and rod tube.

"Morning," I replied, sliding off the porch.

"Well. Did you find the time to practice casting?"

"I did. Every day."

"Oh? Good, then. Let's string 'em up and see how you're doing."

Alton watched me string up my rod as he did the same to his. I was careful not to miss any guides as I threaded the loop of fly line through them.

Alton removed a small box of flies from his vest and walked onto the lawn next to the barn. He stood the box on its end in the grass about thirty feet away and walked back to me. "Okay," he said, "let's see how close to that target you can get your leader."

A test already! It wasn't really a test; I think Alton just wanted to evaluate my casting.

"Let's start with a roll cast," he said.

I flicked some line out from the tip of the rod, made one wave of a false cast to get the line out in front of me, and started; I raised the rod tip straight skyward and as the line looped toward my feet, dropped the rod tip downward. The line did shoot out a bit, but it wasn't a very good roll cast. *Raise my rod higher*, I thought.

I tried another roll cast, but this time, just before I dropped the rod tip toward the fly box target, I raised my casting arm, lifting the rod high into the sky. And this time, the line shot forward better and landed a couple of feet from the box.

"Atta boy!" Alton said. "Again, that roll cast, at least on your creek, will be the most useful cast."

I thought for a moment and replied, "Teri says it's not my creek. It's everybody's creek, and it just happens to run through our farm."

"She's right," he said, "and she's smart. But, I mean, it's the creek you fish almost every day."

I nodded.

He had me casting regular forward-and-backward casts for a few minutes and explained that the practice casts back and forth were called false casts.

"Okay. What do you say we head down to the creek for some chubs."

"Cool!" I replied.

After checking with Mom and letting her know our plans, we cut across the lawn next to the barn and through the bottom field, being careful to step over each mulched row of big pumpkin plants with their tentacle-like vines spreading everywhere, finally stepping over the old rock wall and into the woods beyond. We wove our way past the maples and birches and bulled our way through the alders and young spruce trees to the clearing with my four shelters. I waited for him to say something about them, but he didn't. I noticed the little bark shelter had fallen in upon itself.

I should rebuild that before the fall, I thought. I had a plan to check on the shelters in the winter and see if each of them would keep out the snow.

Alton stepped up to the edge of the creek and motioned me to come closer. He bent down and pointed at a rock half in the water, half on land.

"Have you noticed those before?" he asked.

I knelt on the mossy bank and looked closely. "Yes, I see them all the time. They're dead bugs."

"Well, not really," he said. "They're stonefly casings."

I looked up at him, confused, and then back at the bugs.

"There are no dead bugs there," he continued. "You've seen snake skins that have been shed?"

"Yes."

"These are more like snake sheds but are, more precisely, exoskeletons. Pick one up."

I did, and it disintegrated in my fingers. The word exoskeleton didn't sound good.

Alton continued, "Those casings are what's left behind when a stonefly nymph—that's the stage of life when it lives underwater—crawls out of the water to change into a flying insect. It's one of the times when trout like to eat them. It is sort of like when a snake sheds its skin, but a stonefly does it only once in its life, not every year. It's almost as if the stonefly's shadow is left behind. The adult stonefly will crawl out of the water onto the rocks or plants, emerge from its exoskeleton, then open its wings and fly off to the alders, where it will mate and, sometime after that, will deposit its eggs back into the water. The eggs sink to the bottom and eventually hatch, starting the life cycle all over again."

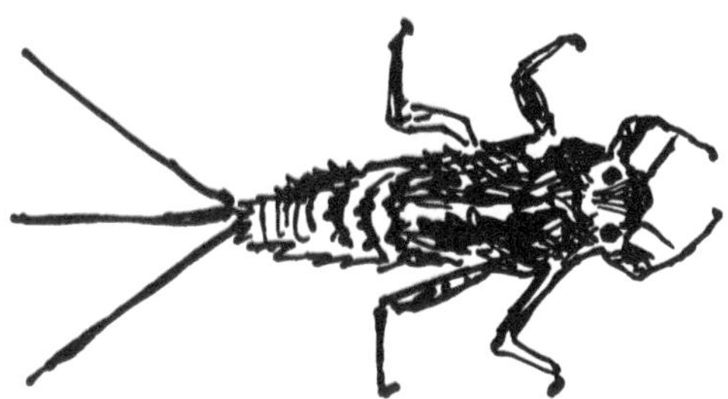

Wow," I said, still staring at the casings all over the rock. I'd seen them a million times but now that I had learned a little about their life-cycle, they looked completely different.

"But there I go," Alton said, "getting way ahead of myself."

Alton then grasped an alder branch and gave it a gentle shake, just as he'd done the first time I saw him. He looked around. "Nothing."

"The caddis flies will start emerging in an hour or so, so let's have a seat for a minute." He pointed to a grassy spot on the bank.

Waving his hand as if over the creek, he said, "Most of what the fish eat is underwater. It depends on whom you ask what percentage, but it doesn't matter. Over time, you'll learn which aquatic insects they eat and at what time of year. But for now, it's enough for you to learn that they exist and that that's what fish eat.

"Around these parts, there are the stoneflies whose skeleton-looking husks you just learned about, but there are many others. Most importantly: caddis flies, mayflies, and midges."

These insect names Al had been using were new to me. He must've sensed it and he waved his hand in front of his chest.

"You don't need to learn them at this point. But I think you should learn a bit about how these insects live and contribute to the fish's food source." He hesitated. "Have I given you too much information already?"

"No, sir," I said.

"Okay," he continued. "Have you ever noticed the many little flies flittering alongside and above the water from spring through fall?"

"Yes, lots of times."

"And have you seen them drop from the sky and touch the water's surface?"

"Yes. It looks like they're thinking about swimming, but they change their minds as soon as their tails hit the water."

Alton laughed. "I suppose that is what it looks like. But, actually, they're dropping their eggs into the water."

I raised my eyebrows. "Oh …"

He nodded and smiled at me and then at the creek. "It's a fascinating new world to learn about, isn't it?"

"Sure is," I said, scanning the air over the creek.

We talked about fish and insects for a while longer, then Alton nudged me with his elbow and pointed at the pool right in front of us. I looked, and within a few seconds, I saw a fish rise and dimple the water's surface on the far side. Then there was another nearby—and another.

"They're probably chubs," Alton declared, "but they're the perfect fish for you to learn fly casting on." He pushed himself up off the rock. "Let's give it a try."

Alton had tied on a little fly he called an Adams. I stepped up to the streambank.

Alton spoke softly. "There are lots of trees and branches here, so you'll have to roll cast. You'll only have to get the fly out about fifteen feet."

I nodded. I pulled some of the fly line from the reel and reached up and grabbed the line near the leader, dragged the slack line through the rod's guides. Repeating the process, I soon had what I figured was enough line out to reach the rising fish.

Alton stood to my left. "Flip the line out into the water. "

I did as he suggested.

"Now, you can roll cast."

I held the rod straight up to the sky with the reel in front of my chest, then raised my arm skyward a bit. The line straightened out in the water and started to loop toward my feet. Then, I dropped the rod with some force. It worked! Just like in the barnyard, the line shot out. It wasn't pretty, but it went far enough to almost reach where the fish had risen. Chubs can be easy to catch, and, with a small splash, one tried immediately to eat the Adams. I jerked the rod tip back, and when I did, I missed the fish, and all the line flew back toward me and balled up at my feet.

"Nice job!" Alton patted me on the left shoulder as I looked at the mess of line in front of me. "We missed him, but that doesn't matter; it was your first cast, and you got the fly where it needed to be. Well done!"

But I knew I'd done something wrong because of the tangled line and said "Arrgh!"

But Alton made me feel proud. I flipped the line back into the water and got ready to try again.

"It's hard to remember at first," Alton offered, "but in fly fishing, the hook set is completely different. We haven't gone over it yet. As soon as the cast hits the water, place the fly line between your right index finger and the rod's grip. Remember? That's how you control the line. You strip the line in with your left hand. As for the hook set, instead of raising the rod tip up and back like with a spinning rod, when a fish hits your fly try to leave your rod tip down, level with the water's surface, and give a quick little strip of the line with your left hand. If you hook him, you'll feel the pressure with your right index finger. But here's the best part: if you miss the fish, instead of the line getting tangled at your feet, the fly will only skitter forward in the water and will still be working for you. Many times, it'll entice the fish to hit it again harder. When bass fishing, you can skitter the fly four or five times on the water in such a way."

I was staring at the line in the water and in my left hand.

"Let's practice it." Alton lowered the rod level, and with his hand on mine, he looped the line under my right pointer finger and then gave quick, short pulls with my left hand.

"I think I got it," I said, and he motioned me to roll cast again.

The second cast was a little better, not perfect, but better. And chubs are never finicky, and a few of them tried taking the fly as soon as it hit the water. I almost raised the rod tip again instinctively but caught myself and left it down. I stripped the fly line, and Alton was right; the fish chased the skittering fly and tried to eat it again and again.

On my third cast, I caught my first fish on a fly rod, a fat little chub about seven inches long. I stripped in the fly line with my left hand until he was close to the bank and I flipped him up onto the moss. Even though it was a chub, which many fishermen called "trash fish," I was thrilled. Alton seemed almost as excited. We stayed in the same spot, and I caught many more chubs, all on a dry fly. As I did, my roll casts got much better. I missed a lot of fish, but Alton patiently helped me with my timing and setting the hook.

After an hour, Alton guided me to a couple of big boulders nearby and we sat down. Al was in his seventies but was tall and thin, and wore khakis, and always looked very cool. When he smoked his pipe—which he never did around us, only when he fished—he looked like the men in photographs from the 1920s.

"Well, what'd you think? Was that fun?"

"It was so much fun," I replied. "If I get better I think I'll be able to catch some trout."

"I have no doubt you will. As I said before, if you practice, you'll improve. You're a good student, Sam."

I was very happy to hear that. My grades at school had always been below average, and it seemed my mind was always wandering when I was in class, no matter how hard I tried to pay attention. Actually, it was the first time I had ever been told I was a good student. Mother always said it was my love of learning that saved me.

"Practice as much as you can, chores permitting." Alton handed me a little box of flies, small enough that the box fit in my pocket. He then snipped off the Adams, which had caught all the chubs, and showed me how to tie it back onto the tip of my leader.

"First, thread the leader through the eye of the hook," Al said, "then pull a couple of inches through and make six or seven wraps of the free end around the leader. Then thread the end back through the little loop you made near the hook's eye. Once you've done that, pull on the leader while carefully holding onto the hook. The knot will tighten up nicely. Then trim off the excess tip with your nail clippers." We repeated it several times until I could tie the knot correctly.

"You'll lose flies once in a while," he said, "in trees, and sometimes fish will break you off. So, this is important to know. Have you got it?"

"Yes, sir."

"Okay. Let's head back to the house. Next Wednesday, we'll practice a forward cast. We'll have to find a spot on the creek clear of branches where you'll have room for a backcast.

We reeled in the line, broke down the rod and placed it into its metal tube. On the walk up to the house, Alton said, "There's a lot to learn. Once you're casting well, we'll go over biology, each week I'll teach you something new—about the fish, what they eat, and the biology of the stream itself."

As Alton drove down the driveway, I sat alone on the porch and took the fly box from my pocket and opened it. *Maybe I am a good student*, I thought. I couldn't wait to get my chores done in the morning and get down to the creek again. And that night, I dreamed of fish splashing at my tiny fly in the water's surface. Tomorrow couldn't come fast enough.

Fourteen

I Receive Mail

I caught more fallfish on Thursday, Friday, and Saturday. After watering the greenhouses, I went into the house for lunch and there was a package on the kitchen table.

"What's that box?" I asked.

Mother slid a bowl of soup in front of me. "No idea," she replied. "It's for you. The return address is from Alton."

My eyes widened, and I pulled the package closer. "I wonder what it is. Feels like a book."

I pulled apart the brown wrapping paper. It *was* a book. I opened it, but the book was empty — no words, no pictures. A small card fell out onto the table. On the front of the card, there was a drawing of a jumping salmon with an insect just in front of its mouth. The card said;

Dear Sam,

It's an honor giving you the gift of fly fishing because, from the sport, you can learn so much. Here is another gift—a journal. You don't have to write in it, of course, but if you choose to, it can be a great learning tool and a way for you to keep track of where and when the fish are biting for future reference.

It can help in other ways, too. When I was your age, I kept a journal, and it often helped me sort out many of life's problems and helped me find answers to things I was curious about. Other times, it just felt good to write things down.

Up to you.

Best,

Alton

"That is very thoughtful," Mother said. "And it's beautiful … the leather cover is pretty, and look, it has a flap that snaps it closed."

"He's right," I said, looking at the salmon, "I have so much to learn from the sport: about the fish, the insects, the fly rod, the line, casting …."

"I think he might've meant something else by that," Mother offered.

I looked at her as she was drying a dish. "Like what?"

"I think he was referring to learning about life. But I could be wrong."

All I knew was that I loved fly fishing already, and I knew I had a lot to learn. As I lay in my bed that night, I wrote in the journal for the first time:

This jernul is from Mr Sanz. I'll try to rite in it.

That afternoon, instead of going down to the creek and roll casting for chubs, I spent a couple of hours practicing full casts in the yard.

The casts were sloppy. I was better at roll casting. I took out the card Alton had given me and looked at the notes and drawings. I could hear Alton's voice in my head; "*Slow everything down if it's not going well.*"

I did slow down the cast, but the line still snapped in the air behind me. *That's right*, I thought, I forgot "*Who cooks for you?*"

With only a dozen more casts there was improvement, especially when I remembered to repeat the owl's call at the top of the backcast. After an hour, I went into the barn, found an old plastic bucket, and made a game of casting practice. I stood the bucket up at the end of the barnyard, maybe forty feet away, and tried to hit it with the leader. Each time I hit it, it was a "base hit." If I could touch the end of the leader *inside* the bucket, it was a home run. I played this game until suppertime.

The following Wednesday, Alton showed up on time again. Mom came out of the greenhouse to say hello.

"Morning, Alton," she said, shielding her eyes from the sun. "How's he doing?"

"Just fine," he replied. "He's at the point now where he just needs to learn some entomology and biology. Then, he'll be off and rolling."

Alton nudged me with his elbow. "Do you have your journal with you?"

"No, just my fishing gear. But I wanted to thank you for the gift."

"You're welcome," he said, "and I did get your thank-you note in the mail. I appreciated that. Why don't you go grab the journal and bring it to the creek? We can make some notes."

"Okay," I said. I ran into the house and stuck the journal in my old canvas backpack with my lunch.

"Let's go catch some fish," he said.

As we picked up our fly rods, Mom said, "Alton, there's a BLT sandwich in his pack for you."

"That's mighty kind of you, Rachel."

Mother waved and walked back toward the greenhouse, and Alton and I started making our way across the fields to the creek. As we stepped between the planted rows, he said, "Do you know the word entomology?"

I didn't have to think about it. "No idea."

"Well, today, after we work on casting a little, we're going to learn about insects."

"Oh, good. I like bugs."

Alton and I found a spot on the creek where there was room enough behind me to make some regular forward casts, and he watched me pull a dry fly out of my fly box.

"A Royal Wulff—good choice. How are you coming with tying the tippet onto the leader?" he asked before I started.

"I think I've got that," I replied. "I practiced it the day after my first lesson."

"Okay then, let's see your clinch knot to tie the fly on."

In my left hand, I held the fly by its tiny hook and threaded the thin tippet through the eye. I then folded about an inch-and-a-half of the tippet back upon itself, repositioned my left thumb and pointer finger to hold the hook's eyelet and the loop of tippet, and wrapped the short end of tippet around the long end five or six times, making a small loop next to the hook's eye. Then, I pulled the tag of tippet back through the small loop and pulled the leader and the fly against each other gently, cinching the whole thing down, tightening the knot into the eyelet.

"Excellent," Alton said. "Now, this section of tippet material I gave you is what's called 5-x. That's how the manufacturers label the diameters of tippet: 4-x, 5-x, 6-x, and so on. The larger the number, the smaller the diameter, which means the less strong the tippet is. For the fishing you'll do in this creek, 5-or 6-x is all you'll need. If you go fishing specifically for bass, you might want some 3-or 4-x."

I began wondering how I would ever buy some more tippet—or where to buy it, but Alton answered that question.

"I have many extra spools of different sizes, and I'll leave some with you today."

"Thank you."

"You're welcome. That's enough tippet talk for now. Let's see if you can catch something in this pool."

I pulled from my pocket a pair of nail clippers and snipped off the tail from my newly tied clinch knot.

I faced the creek, pulled some line off the reel, flicked the fly line, leader, tippet and fly into the water at my feet and made a little roll cast just to get the line out a bit more. When I made my first backcast and the line was lifting off the water, I noticed a couple of chubs were trying for the fly already. But the deeper section of the pool was twenty-five feet from the streambank. I made extra sure I didn't go too far back with the flyrod—maybe I went to the 1 or 2 o'clock position and paused.

Down went the rod tip, and out shot the line. It was a nearly perfect cast. Immediately a fat chub rose with a splash and took the fly. With my left hand, I stripped back the fly line, securing it between my right pointer finger and the rod, and pulled in the first fish of the day.

"Well done, Sam!" Alton gently slapped my left shoulder. He seemed almost excited. "Very nice cast. And I liked the little roll cast to get yourself started. I think you've got it. You've obviously been practicing."

I felt a strange sense of accomplishment. I was always more

comfortable and confident when doing things in the out-of-doors, but this was different. In that moment, seeing how happy Alton was with my progress, I suddenly felt like I could do…I don't know…*more.*

I was quite proud, and pride was not something I had remotely thought of as I tied on the Wulff a few minutes earlier.

I caught a dozen or so more chubs from the same spot, while Alton fine-tuned my casting technique. I hadn't had that much fun in a long time.

"All right," Alton said. "Let's find a place to sit near the water. We'll talk bugs."

Fifteen

I Learn About Insects & Other Things

Alton sat next to me on the same rock.

"You have already learned some things about stoneflies when we looked at their casings weeks ago. Do you remember?"

"I think so," I said, squinting up at him. "They swim, sprout wings, then they find a wife."

Alton smiled and almost laughed. The guy was always smiling at stuff I said, but not in a weird way. Either I was funnier than I realized, or I said some pretty dumb stuff. I didn't care. He was the best teacher I'd ever had. My only worry was that I wouldn't learn fast enough, and he'd get frustrated.

"That's close enough," Alton responded. "I have an idea. What do you think about taking some notes in your journal? That way, if you can't remember anything we talk about, you can refer back to this day and go over what you learned. It's entirely up to you."

I removed two bottles of soda pop and the journal and pencil from my backpack. "I'll try," I said. "I don't write very good—*well.*"

"That's okay," he said. "I didn't write well either when I was your age. Keeping the journal going will be good practice. Besides, this journal is just for you. It doesn't have to be Shakespeare. Any mistakes you make in your journal won't matter. No one will ever grade it."

I opened it up to where the duct tape was and picked up the pencil.

"You might want to date your entries," he continued, "in case you do ever want to look something up in the future. It's good practice to always date the page. Again, it's up to you."

I wrote the date at the top-left of the page.

May 21, 1972

I stared at the blank page and got that old familiar feeling whenever I had to write anything. Not sick, really, but uneasy in my stomach.

Without looking up at him, I said, "I don't know how to do it."

"That's okay. Why don't I help you with the first couple of lines, and then you'll get the idea."

"Okay." I was still staring at the page. "But I write slow."

"All right. Let's start with this;"

I wrote it down just as he said it, but it took longer than it should've: *I am siting on a big roc next to the creek that is neer my sheltr. This morng, I cawt some chubs on a Royl Wulf and we are going to disgus insecs.*

I could see Alton watching me out of the corner of his eye, and again he patted me on the shoulder. He said, "That's fine. Just fine."

"Let's just talk about the insects, and you can write what you want now, or you can write down your thoughts about them when you're home tonight—as you remember the conversation. One way is as good as the other."

Alton leaned into a small bush and nudged a small insect onto his hand and presented it to me. It was a black and yellow beetle.

"On second thought," he said, "why don't you start your journal with some drawings?"

I readied my pencil and inspected the beetle.

"Skip a page, why don't you?"

I looked up at him and did as he asked. The insect's antennae were as long as its body, so I started with them. Then, I sketched the outline of the body and added the legs.

"Good," Al said. "Now, let's give it some context."

I squinted at the journal.

"Go back a page."

I did as he said.

"I think it would be fun to draw a simple map to show where we found this little beast." Al pointed across and upstream. "That's north. In the upper right corner of the page, draw a straight line about an inch long in the same direction as my finger."

I did. It was angled toward the top and to the right of the page.

"Perfect. Now, make the top end of the line an arrow."

I drew that.

"And now, write the letter 'N.'

"See? Now you can sketch a little map and show where we're sitting. Using your mind's eye, we know your house and barn are directly behind us. First, draw the two big maples between here and the house, then the old rock wall curving along the bottom field. After that, you'll know where to draw the creek."

I did it all. It took a few minutes, but it didn't look too bad. What amazed me was that it looked pretty darned accurate. I even included the clearing with my shelter.

I left the journal open and kept the pencil ready but didn't write much more.

"Now," he continued, "the fish in this creek eat many things, but today we're going to concentrate on the flying insects other than stoneflies that live under the water for parts of their life: mayflies, caddis flies, and midges. Let's start with the mayflies."

That night, I wrote everything I could remember in my journal. Mother helped me with spelling and I made some sketches. It was fun to do it together in front of the fireplace.

Today Alton told me abut meny of the inseks fish eat. First wer Mayflies, that we saw flying above the creek. He told me things like about half of an insek's body is its abdomen and that mayflies, kaddis flies, and many other inseks that live under water have their gills lokated on the sides of their bellys.

Mother helped me with the rest. I told her what I learned, and she wrote the words, then she tried to explain the spelling of each word:

Alton said that of all the insects imitated by fly fishermen and fly tiers over the years, the mayfly is the "favorite." Their delicate wings stick upright and are easier to see both in the air and the water. They are also delicate looking and can be pretty—both while flying and floating downstream.

Most mayflies live underwater in a nymph or larval stage for about a year until they emerge from the water to a winged stage to mate and lay eggs. Before they hit the surface, the nymphs shuck their outer skin, like the stoneflies do on the rocks. Alton said it's amazing that the mayflies emerge, mate, and drop their eggs back into the stream all in less than twenty-four hours—some in only a few hours.

When the time and conditions are right, the mayfly nymphs float or swim to the surface, shucking their "skin," then float in the current for a bit while they unfold their wings, letting them dry before flying off into the bushes along the stream banks. At some point, either in the air or in the bushes, the mayflies mate. Then, they drop their eggs into the stream where they sink to the bottom, then the parent insects die. The life cycle begins again.

There are several life stages that Alton says are important to fly fishermen, but he said I can learn them later. And he said there are many types of mayflies.

Caddis flies, Al said, are more complicated than mayflies. He also thinks they are more interesting. They have a pupa stage, and many caddis larvae build little houses for themselves, called "cases."

I asked for the pencil and added a line at the end:

Al is gong to teech my more next weak.

Mother used the pencil and pointed out some of my words. "See, Honey, how you spelled 'caddis' with a k—'kaddis?' Remember your vowels?"

I recited them to her.

"Good." She picked up a piece of scrap paper and wrote down the letters as she explained. "Al suggested we go over this; so, the letters 'C' and 'K' can be used to spell the same sound, but 'K' is used before the letters e, i, or y. The letter 'C' is used before a, o, u, and consonants. There's no certain rule for the double 'D' in caddis, I know…it's weird, but if you spell it and read it enough times, you'll memorize it."

Then, she had me write the same words on the scrap paper.

"Well done, Sam!"

"Mom," I asked. "Can we go to the library after school tomorrow? I want to see if there are any books on mayflies."

"Teri is picking you up tomorrow, and I'm sure she won't mind. I'll call her just in case."

"Thanks Mom, for helping me with the writing in the journal. I know I'm not good at writing."

"You're welcome. It was fun. And don't worry; you'll get better with time. I'm glad you're doing it. And I've told you before how proud I am of you for trying to read books as much as you do. It's so good for you."

I shook my head. "I learn best from the pictures, like in my Scout book."

"That doesn't matter, Honey, as long as you continue to try to read as much as you can and learn what you can."

Over the next few weeks, Alton and I walked the creek and fished. Twice he asked permission from Mother to go farther upstream and we caught some nice brook trout. My first trout I caught on a fly was a keeper, but Alton made me release it. I wanted to bring it home to Mother to eat.

I removed the tiny fly from its lip and looked at it admiringly. I held the dark, spotted little fish as it gulped hard, trying to breathe. I was excited and didn't think about it suffocating.

"Sam, now let him go."

I looked up at Alton. "But …"

"Let him go," he said softly.

I reached down and unceremoniously dropped the fish into the water and watched him swim away.

"You wanted to keep it, didn't you?" Alton said.

"Mom likes to eat trout a *lot.*"

"I understand, but I think releasing your first trout caught on a fly was a good thing. Maybe it's good karma. Do you know what karma is?"

I shook my head.

"Well, in a nutshell, your actions — all the little things you do — have results in the universe. And the things that happen to you or for you in the future might have something to do with your past actions. If you do good things regularly, good things might happen to you in the future, or vice-versa; if you do bad things, bad stuff may come your way down the line. Now, keeping that little trout to eat would not be a bad thing, but isn't it nice to let him live? It doesn't hurt to be kind to living things. That said, I do keep a few for dinner once in a while."

"I think I get it," I said.

"And besides," Alton said, "wouldn't it be fun to catch him again in a year or two when he's twice as big?"

"Sure would."

We continued to fish and caught a few more trout, with Alton fine-tuning my casting. On the way back to the house, he talked about insect hatches and explained when it was better to fish with caddis flies instead of mayflies or stoneflies.

Halfway home, we sat on a big boulder, and Al helped me write down some of the insect lessons he had just given me. He was even more patient than Mother. I told him so, and he said he had been a teacher for thirty-eight years.

He pointed at a caddis fly as it shucked its casing, dried its wings for a second and, breaking out of the water's surface film, flew off. "For all those years," he said, "I watched students emerge from high school. Sometimes it was hard to let them go. They'd spread their wings, and while some would make good life decisions, some didn't." He looked down at my journal.

When I tried to write 'the caddis has a tan body,' I misspelled the word caddis *again*. Alton wrote the word and had me sound it out. Then,

I recognized it and spelled it correctly. He did that with different words. As I said, he was *very* patient.

Then we closed the journal, stood up, and picked up the fly rods.

"Let's go see if your mom has time to take a lunch break," Al said.

A moment later, he said, "It's almost Memorial Day. The smallmouth bass are spawning. If we can hit them at the right time, you'll be in for a treat."

Sixteen
WE GET AN IDEA

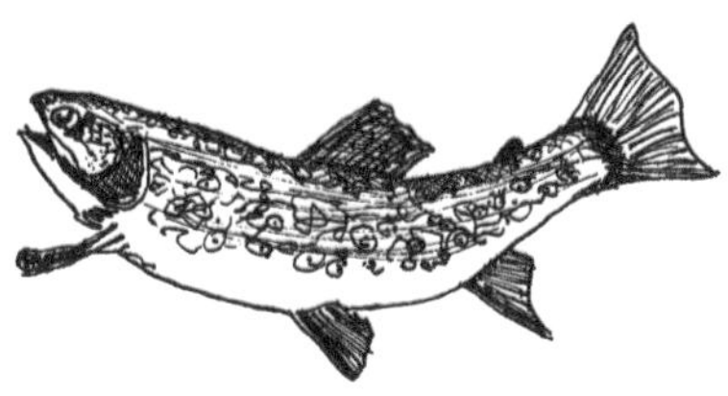

When we got home, Mother was stepping out of greenhouse No. 2.

"Any luck, you two?"

"Yes!" I replied. "You would have loved it; we caught six trout, all on dry flies."

I saw her look me over. My hands were empty.

"We let them go," I told her. "It's just good karma."

I saw her smile at Alton as she wiped sweat and potting soil from her forehead.

"Well, that's good," she said, "maybe you'll have even better luck next time."

"Exactly," I said.

"Can you stay for lunch, Alton? We have some homemade chicken stew that Teri and I made last night."

"Rachel, I'd love to," Alton said. "Sounds great."

Al seemed to love the stew and Mom gave him some bread and butter from one of the loaves she baked last Sunday, which made it two days old, but it was still very good.

I think Mom liked that Al was enjoying the meal. "Why don't you come over for dinner this Sunday, when the bread will be fresh?"

"That's kind of you Rachel, but I'd hate to intrude."

Mother put her hand on Al's shirtsleeve. "It would never be an intrusion. But I must warn you, I don't know what will be served at this point. Over the past year, Teri has gotten into cooking and experimenting with sometimes exotic meals. And I've started taking an interest in it also. Lately, we all three have been preparing meals together on the weekends." She paused for a moment, and then asked, "Do you like to cook, Alton?"

"I used to enjoy it, when my wife was alive. Years ago, Alice met Julia Child in Cambridge when she was at a conference there. They hit it off, and Alice ended up with her famous cookbook. We tried getting through all of the recipes in it, and if it weren't for one funny disaster with Coq au Vin, we might've made it."

"I'd like to hear that story," Mother said.

Alton looked a little sad for a moment, swallowed his bite of bread and said, "No, that story is just for me, I reckon." Then he smiled at Mom. "I'll tell you what," he continued. "Why don't you check with Teri and see if she has anything planned for this Sunday. If not, then I'll come prepared for one of the meals we made that did come out pretty well, and we all can have a hand in it. And I'll tell a different story while we cook."

I think Mother could see that I was excited about the idea of Al coming for Sunday dinner, and she answered, "I think that's a great idea. I'll check and call you before Friday. Would that give you enough time to get the ingredients?"

"If you could call by Thursday that would be better. I look forward to Sunday whether I cook or not."

"Great," Mom replied, "but why don't you come around noon? Even if Teri does have something planned, you can help with the cooking. It's a big farmhouse kitchen, as you can see. There's plenty of room for lots of cooks."

I didn't see Al the rest of the week. I fished on Friday and caught a boatload of chubs on a size 16 Royal Wulff dry fly. When Sunday morning arrived, it was a rainy, grey day. Mother had called Al and told him the meal was his choice, and that Teri was looking forward to cooking with him.

Al arrived in his old Jeep right on time. I saw him coming and went out on the porch to welcome him. He motioned me to the Jeep.

"Hi, Sam. Be a champ and carry these two bags for me?"

He handed me the bags from the back seat. He carried a big cooler up onto the porch and placed it next to the door.

"What are we having?" I asked.

Al shot me a big smile, grabbed the lid of the cooler and said, "You ready for this?"

I'd never seen him smile so wide. He lifted the lid and lying on ice were two of the biggest fish I'd ever seen. They were beautiful—silvery, perfectly proportioned, and they had black spots here and there along their bodies. Both were over twenty inches long. I couldn't imagine catching them, but I tried.

"Wow!" is all I could say.

"Wow, indeed. Salmon. I caught them yesterday afternoon far up the big river and immediately cleaned them streamside and packed them in ice."

"What'd you catch them on?"

"A little size eighteen caddis fly. It took some doing to land them."

"I bet it did. Tell me about it!"

"How about after supper? There's a lot to do to cook them."

I looked at the salmon again.

Alton went back to the Jeep and retrieved a huge pan with a lid on it and set it next to the cooler.

"Didn't know if your Mom has a big pan like this."

The door opened and Mother stepped onto the porch in her apron.

"Right on time," she smiled.

"Mom! Look what Alton caught." I waited for Al to open the cooler. "He got them up the big river!"

"Oh, my," Mother exclaimed. "How exciting."

Mom looked happy. I had heard her say more than once that she couldn't afford salmon. Now, here were two big, wild ones.

"I'm prepared to poach them in a creamy lemon garlic butter sauce," Al said.

Mother must love salmon because she forgot her normal reserved self and gave Al a quick hug.

Alton chuckled and said, "Well, you haven't tasted it yet."

"Oh, I'm sure they'll be wonderful."

Teri drove in and after bounding up the steps she gave Al a hug.

"Sorry," Teri exclaimed, "I'm a hugger."

Al chuckled at Teri's outwardness. "The pleasure's all mine."

As everyone settled into the kitchen and started cooking, I set the table for four. I sat and listened to the grownups talk about food and cooking. It was nice. Mother always told me my Dad would sometimes say, "Too many cooks in the kitchen," but that certainly didn't seem the case. All three seemed to get along great, each one learning cooking tips from the others. Alton had brought a hand-written recipe.

"It's from Julia's book," he said. "One of my wife's favorite dishes. Are either of you experienced in poaching salmon?"

"I've tried several times, years ago," Teri replied, "but I was disappointed each time. So, from a practical standpoint, no."

"Alice was very good at it, thanks to Julia. So, let's see how it goes."

Mother touched Teri's shoulder. "I nearly forgot to tell you; Al's wife Alice met Julia Child."

"No way."

Al nodded at her.

"That's so cool," Teri said. "I'm a fan."

Alton opened a cupboard door and slipped the recipe under the bottom and closed the door so that it hung down where everyone could read it.

"Teri," he said, "once the fish go into the oven, would you be in charge of the lemon garlic butter sauce? You can use the recipe here at the end of the page or make your own, whichever you choose."

"Happy to."

"Shall I poach the fish then?" he asked.

"Of course," both women replied.

"I'm just following the recipe," Al said. "Just as Alice and I did from

Julia's book. Let's begin. The oven needs to be the proper temperature range, or we will ruin the fish very quickly. Salmon is a delicate protein, so we need to cook it very gently. But first, these are too big for the pan, so I'll take the heads off."

Using big scissors, Al cut off the heads right through the bones, then the fins, but left the tails on. Then, he reached into one of his grocery bags and shoved some parsley, dill, and tarragon into the fish's bellies.

"Salmon has a fantastic flavor," he said, "but I want to introduce some extra tastes. These herbs will enhance the flavor of the fish, but not overpower it." Then he cut some slices of lemon and put three in each belly with the herbs.

"Rachel, could you preheat the oven to 380 degrees, please?"

Alton pulled out two huge pieces of aluminum foil. He smeared butter over each piece and made beds on both with the rest of the herbs and added a few more slices of lemon. He added some black peppercorns into the fish, and some sea salt. I had never given cooking much thought, but it was fun to watch them. Al then placed both fish onto the pieces of foil, and then he rolled two small pieces of aluminum foil into about the shape and size of hot dogs. He shoved one into each fish's belly.

"This will give the fish some structure as it cooks," he said. "It'll also make filleting them once they're cooked a great deal easier."

"Interesting," Teri said.

"This might be different, too," Al said. "We'll cook the salmon upright on the beds of herbs, oriented just as if they were swimming. Could you each roll the foil up and wrap the fish, leaving a little opening where the heads were?"

While Mom and Teri wrapped the fish, Al took a bottle out of a bag and opened it. He poured out two cups of wine, one for each fish.

As he poured it into the foil openings, he said, "This is just to add a bit of moisture. It'll help steam the fish while adding another dimension of flavor." Then he sealed the foil of each. He put them in the big baking pan and placed them in the oven.

Alton clapped his hands once. "That's it for preparation. Nothing to it. Now we make the sauce. They'll be ready in about thirty minutes. But here …" Al reached back into a bag. "I have some rice to start now, and some green beans from my garden."

"Al, we could've supplied veggies," Mother said.

"Happy to do it," Alton replied. "I think you'll like these Kentucky Blue Lake beans. They're great."

Everyone busily kept chopping, talking, and cooking while the fish were in the oven. When they finished cooking, Alton unwrapped the foil and the wonderful smell of salmon and herbs filled the kitchen. It was clear to the three of us that Al did still enjoy cooking.

"We have to peel the skin off while the fish are hot," he said. "Rachel, do you have two sharp knives?" Mother handed him one and got ready to skin the second fish.

"Starting up by where the dorsal fins were, we need to start scraping the skin off." Al peeled it off pretty easily. There were some darker sections of the flesh, and Al scrapped that off, too, leaving only the pretty, pink meat. Mother did the same.

Just as Teri said, "The rice and beans are ready," Al re-covered one of the skinned fish with aluminum foil, and the other he gently lifted from the pan using two spatulas and placed on a serving dish. He poured some of the lemon butter sauce over the fish, and we sat down to eat. Mother said Grace, as she always did, and thanked Alton for the wonderful fish.

"Oh, my God," Teri mumbled with a bite of the salmon in her mouth, "this is *so* good."

I like catching fish more than just about anything else, but it's not one of my favorite foods. But this meal was excellent. After the meal, we cleaned the kitchen and all went into the front living room. Mother showed Alton some photos, the grandfather clock, and the painting of my father flyfishing that hangs over the couch. It used to be over the fireplace mantle, but Teri made Mom move it because she said it would get damaged by the soot from the fires.

"This is the painting I told you about in the greenhouse. I love it."

Alton stood in front of the painting for a long moment. Then he said simply, "It's nice. From my memory, it does look like Jody, how he stood in the river."

"You knew Jody?" Teri asked.

Alton turned toward her. "I met him fishing a few times, up on the West Branch of the river. Jody was a popular guy. We spoke some." Then he turned from the painting and found a chair to settle into.

I couldn't hold it in any longer. "Alton, tell me about catching the salmon?"

"Please," Mother said to me.

"Sorry … Please tell us."

"One of the fish was interesting, but I doubt your Mom and Teri want to hear the story."

"Of course we do," both women spoke at once.

"All right then," Al said. "I'll tell it, but I fear it's not that great a story."

Seventeen

I Learn About Salmon

Alton settled back into the big, overstuffed chair next to the fireplace, and Mother and I found the couch. Teri, as usual, grabbed a throw pillow and plopped down onto the braided rug. She liked sitting on the floor for some reason.

"Al," Mother said, "You must take some of the second fish home with you. We'll eat some of it tomorrow, but I couldn't stand for any of it to go to waste."

"Happy to," Al replied.

"Alton," I said, "those were the biggest fish I've ever seen."

"You aren't obliged to tell stories," Mom interjected. She looked at me. "Maybe Al just wants to digest his supper."

"No, no," Alton said. "I'm always happy to talk about fly fishing."

"What you need to know," he said, settling into a story, "is that almost everything about fishing for salmon is different than what you're used to. Make no mistake, Sam, you are extremely lucky to have Dibbin Creek running through your land, and you know how much we both love it, but the big river where the salmon are is something else. This land is all farmland. When we walk down to the creek, the banks are crowded with small willows and alders. In the summer, we see arrowhead and three types of fern, along with cardinal flowers and wild asters. And in the quiet, shallow parts of the creek, we see water lilies and pickerelweed. But except for the big maples along the rock wall, there isn't much in the way of great timber. This land has been worked and harvested for many generations.

"But the salmon rivers are in the great North Woods. The river I fished yesterday—the Sebatekew River—is *not* like your creek. The river is choked on both sides with fine stands of birch, spruce, and beech. There are oaks, ash, red maple, white pine, wild cherry, cedar, and the occasional locust scattered among them. The river is deep, wild, and dangerous. In your creek, there's always the danger of slipping in and getting wet, but if you can swim, you'd just be wet and cold and you'd have to go home. In the rushing, roiling, rapids of the Sebatekew, you can die. It is a place that demands respect."

It was a great story. To me, the North Woods had always sounded like a magical place.

"It's important to wade the river," Al continued, "to get free from the trees so you'll have a backcast, but there are only certain spots you can safely do that. You have to know the water. I bet I made a dozen trips, just watching other flyfishers until I learned which spots I could venture into.

"When I got to the river yesterday, there were alderflies all over the branches along the bank." He glanced at me. "That's a type of caddis fly. There were a few fish rising, taking little sips in the water's surface, so I pulled from my box a small size eighteen elk hair caddis which I tie especially for the Sebatekew; I hoped it would work."

"I have some of those you gave me," I interjected.

"That's right," Alton smiled. "The pool I chose to fish is sometimes called The Ledges Pool. It's pretty close to the road but holds some big fish." I saw Mother glance up at the painting of father. Al continued, "I've hooked and lost a few salmon in there that were about six pounds. Some large brook trout are in there, also. It's impossible to wade out very far in that pool—it's too deep close to the bank.

"There are ledges at the pool, as the name implies, at the head of it. I learned long ago that I couldn't wade up at the head; there it's too dangerous. So I started at the downriver end of the pool and began casting up and across the current. With only the second cast, a good-sized fish made a pass at my fly but didn't eat it. A few casts later, I moved opposite the middle of the pool. Still, I could only wade out about ten feet. Any farther and I risked stepping off a submerged boulder and taking a dip over my head. Wearing waders, they could fill up with water and I could drown. So, ten feet out, I found some good footing and made some casts."

I was loving this story. I closed my eyes, imagining the scene. Teri reached for another pillow and made herself more comfortable.

"There were trees only a few feet behind me, so I had to roll cast."

I thought it was cool that I knew what Al was talking about—that I knew all about roll casts.

"And they had to be good roll casts," Al continued. "I had to get out about forty feet of line. I could see where the feeding lanes were in the seams next to the faster water in the middle of the river. I spotted fish sipping at the water's surface in the seam and some of the fish were porpoising, which told me they were going for emerging insects."

Al was looking at me. "Do you remember the emerging state of the caddis and mayfly's life cycles?"

I nodded.

"Good." Alton went on with his story. "So, I snipped off the Parachute Adams I had started with and tied on that caddis fly I told you about. Since it looked like the fish were feeding just barely under the surface, I planned on fishing it 'wet,' letting the fly sink an inch or so. I flipped the fly into the current at my feet, payed out some more line, and made my roll cast. It was a good one. The line unfurled and delivered the fly a little upriver from where the fish were rising, right into the feeding lane. I didn't see a fish take my fly, but the line acted strangely, and in an instant, I realized a fish had taken the fly just as it hit the water! I stripped in one arm's length of line quickly and raised the rod tip slightly and I felt the fish. I could tell it was a good one. It felt heavy right away. It came right at me and I had to strip in line with my left hand to take up any slack. When he — it looked like a male to me — got closer he must've seen me. He jumped three feet out of the water, twice. I could see he was over twenty inches and fat. He then sounded into a deep hole right in front of me. He sat still on the bottom. I knew I'd hooked him well, and that gave me time to reel in all the slack line. Once I had him on the reel, I could play him with the reel's drag."

"What happened next?" I asked.

"I adjusted my drag, dropped the rod tip pointing it right at him in the hole, and with my left hand I stripped a little line between the rod and my right index finger, just like I've shown you. I had to move him out of his spot on the river's bottom. He hated that! He took off in a flash toward the current in the middle of the river. He shot into the air, turned end-over-end, and landed on his side with a huge splash, leaped again, falling on his back, and then skidded off into the rapids. He was magnificent. The drag was whining and the tippet at the end of the leader was strained—I was sure of that. Now, remember, I was standing on an underwater boulder. I couldn't move from my spot. I would risk taking a dip, so that meant I couldn't follow him downriver if he chose that route. I'd have to play him from where I stood. I wasn't sure if the tippet would break or not. All I could do was try to play him with some finesse."

I looked at Mother and Teri. They were both listening to the story, staring at Al.

"It seemed like minutes went by," Alton continued. "The fish kept running, sulking, and doing everything a salmon can think of to get loose. Eventually, the fish became exhausted and rolled quietly on its side about five feet from my net. I raised my rod tip and dragged him gently toward my legs and slipped the net under him. He barely fit, with his head and tail protruding above the net's wooden rim.

"I caught and released several smaller fish before catching the second one I kept." Al lifted a finger toward the kitchen. "The one in your refrigerator. It too was fun to catch but was in easier water to fish, and not as tough a fight as the first. I eventually threaded my way through the alders and worked my way back to the car. I drove home after dark and thought over the day. I tell you, I don't know how many days I have left of fishing the big rivers, but I sure do savor every one of them now."

Mother chimed in. "And we had a great time cooking him."

Alton smiled at her. "Yes. The perfect meal with finest company."

"Well, Al," Teri said, slapping the arm of her chair, "you're now a part of this small, weird family if that suits you. You're welcome anytime."

Alton looked taken aback for a moment, but, after an awkward pause, said, "I'd be honored."

Over the summer, Alton did become more and more like family. He came to the farm more frequently, teaching me more advanced flyfishing, and about all the things that seventy-three years of observing life and nature had taught him.

I did not know then what a remarkable summer it would be.

Eighteen
We Build for the Future

For the first time in my life, I had to learn to manage my time. Alton first arranged things with Mother, and he started visiting the farm several times a week. I looked forward to our times down by the creek learning, observing nature, and catching fish so much that I was motivated to get my chores done early each morning. I think the nature lessons were my favorite part of my time with Al.

One day, as we made our way to the creek, we stopped and looked at the shelters I had built earlier in the spring. The Tepee and the smaller Wickiup had fallen down, but the rest remained standing. The Adirondack still looked usable. Al walked around it. I hoped he was admiring it. I was proud of my first real construction job. In the time since I built it, I had learned how to fly fish, much about plants, animals, birds, and even conservation. I was starting to feel, I don't know, *older*. Looking into the Adirondack shelter, it felt like I'd built it years ago.

"Very nice," Al said.

"Thank you. I slept in it one night, right after I finished it. Mom slept over there," I said, pointing across the clearing, "in her tent. I could hear her crying in the night."

As soon as it came out of my mouth I was angry for saying that. Alton didn't need to know that. Sometimes things just came out of my mouth when I talked to people, and I didn't know why.

Al nodded, looked away, and said, "Sometimes it feels good to cry and let things out. It's helpful."

"I suppose so," I replied. "Anyway, Mom and I spoke that night, and she said she and my Dad had talked about someday building a little cabin here to use as a sort of camp on summer nights."

"That'd be nice," he said. Al looked up into the trees surrounding the clearing. He walked twenty feet this way, and forty feet another way and peered upstream and then down. Then he walked to the edge of the clearing away from the creek to where tiny, three-foot-high saplings grew in a swatch. Then he walked back to my shelter. I wondered what he was doing.

"Let's go check out the creek."

"Okay," I said.

We walked to the edge of the water and stood on the bank of the pool where I caught my first chub on a fly. That too seemed like long ago. Then I saw some movement in the pool. A large eel came swimming slowly upstream, and I became mesmerized by it.

"What a weird animal," I said.

"Weird? The common eel?" Alton asked.

I looked up at him, then back at the eel, wriggling through the pool. I once held one that I caught accidentally, and the smooth, slimy skin creeped me out. "Yup," I said. "Weird."

"They're different from most other fish," Al said, "but I think they're fascinating—not strange. On second thought, they're incredible creatures."

"Incredible?"

"Indeed. They begin their existence as an egg deposited in the depths of the Atlantic Ocean somewhere southeast of Bermuda. When the egg matures, it floats slowly toward the surface. Soon after, the tiny eel, flat, colorless, and transparent sets out with multitudes of companions on the long voyage to the continents.

"The American and European eels differ in the number of vertebrae in their spines; otherwise, they're indistinguishable, but the tiny European eels all head for Europe, and the American eels swim for our rivers, streams and creeks." Al pointed into the pool. "Like Dibbin Creek."

"When they reach the brackish water of our river estuaries—our bays where the rivers reach the ocean—the eels become yellowish-brown in color and take on a more snakelike form. Most of the males probably remain in the bays and river mouths, but the females, which, just like in the human race, are usually the toughest of most species, keep traveling far inland, up the tiniest of streams and creeks, even wiggling overland over dewy grass … even dropping into culverts and drainpipes. They squirm over dams, and over seemingly insurmountable obstacles to reach the lakes and ponds where they will grow to maturity over a period of four to five years."

It was one of those many moments when I realized I would never be as smart as Alton.

Al continued. "About the fifth year in the lake or pond, the spawning urge is stimulated by their endocrine system, and the females journey back down to the estuaries where they're greeted by the waiting, excited males. Together, they all swim back to that single spot in the Atlantic to spawn and die.

"Weird?" Al said. "I think they're extraordinary, but I don't think I'd want to eat one."

Al looked down at me and we both wrinkled our noses. Then we walked upstream to look for rising fish.

As we stepped through the fern and the alders, Al said, "People do though—eat them. The folks in the Far East love them."

"I'll pass," I said.

He stopped and turned back to me. "As long as you know that it's very important to try different things as you go through life; if you don't, you might never learn what you're passionate about. A life without passion is fruitless."

Then he kept walking.

We walked far enough upstream that we caught some small brook trout. By now, Mother and Al had talked many times, and she trusted Al with me. She knew I'd never get lost while with him, and she knew Al would never let anything happen to me. I was very happy to occasionally leave the big maples and fish for trout.

We did not keep any that day. Al told me for the umpteenth time that if we harvested trout on each trip, a creek as small as ours might get fished out, and there'd be too few or no fish to catch in future years. It made perfect sense to me. We gently released all we caught.

On the way home, as we wound our way along the creek, something caught Al's eye. An enormous snapping turtle was submerged in about a foot of water close to the bank. I had never seen one so large; its shell was about a foot-and-a-half in diameter. Alton squatted to get a closer look. I knelt next to him.

"Just like the eels," he said, "snapping turtles are also amazing creatures."

"Do they go down to the ocean too?" I asked. The only thing I knew about snapping turtles was I shouldn't touch them.

"No." Alton almost chuckled but stopped himself. "See how wide her shell, or carapace is? At least it *looks* like a 'she,' but I can't tell."

"I see it."

"That's a good sixteen, maybe seventeen inches across. I bet she's nearly a hundred years old. Think of it; she might've been here in this creek when Custer was getting wiped out at the Little Big Horn."

"Wow," I said.

"Yeah … wow."

Alton tossed his dry fly a little upstream and caught a six-inch chub. He killed it and tossed it near the turtle which was still submerged. The splash made the ancient thing twitch and its head retracted into its shell but only for a moment. It turned toward the floating dead chub and stared suspiciously at it for a long time. Al and I sat on the bank to see what the snapping turtle would do. Would she eat the fish? Drag it away?

The old reptile finally moved and grabbed the chub and pulled it underwater.

It took her forty-five minutes to eat the fish, grasping it with its hooked beak then awkwardly pushing against it with its claws until a chunk of the carcass was torn free. She would lie still for a minute before making a sudden gulp and swallowing. The turtle never came up for air. Oddly, the old snapper left the head of the chub. When it had finished eating Al's gift, it finally surfaced. She sat in the water with half of her head sticking out. It looked at me with its cold little eyes; I could see each pupil was a perfect cross. Then, it simply submerged, turned, and slipped off into the depths of the pool.

"I have a lot of respect for snapping turtles," Alton said. "They've evolved to be well suited for most environmental changes, yet they haven't changed much over the millennia. In the spring, when turtles are crossing busy roads to find gravel banks to lay their eggs in, I drive around in the mornings to pick them up and help them to the roadsides. There are people who try to hit them and kill them on purpose when they see snapping turtles on the road."

"What? Why?" I asked.

"Because they're ignorant. I know that's a harsh word, but it's true in this sense. Some folks are ignorant of how important these aquatic creatures are to the watershed. The eels we saw—they're ugly, but they're important too. These turtles, they eat all the things in the water that have died. They clean the streams, creeks and rivers of things that would decay on the bottom. Decaying animal and vegetable matter sucks oxygen from the water."

Al gave me a chance to offer something, but I couldn't think of anything.

"What needs lots of oxygen in the water to survive?"

I thought hard for a moment. "Trout!"

"You got it. All fish, actually, but trout and salmon need a lot of oxygen. See how all the creatures in the creek contribute to a healthy stream?"

"Yes, sir," I replied.

"Next time, we'll talk about how drastically the old hydroelectric dams damaged the ecosystems."

Alton tossed his chin at the creek. "These snapping turtles, they have an air of the ancient about them. They were living in the ooze of prehistoric riverbeds for many centuries before mammals ever raised their heads above the fern."

Alton looked at me. "Did you know that mammals arrived in the Triassic Period, about 252 million to 201 million years ago, and derived from members of the reptilian order Therapsida?"

I had no idea what he was talking about. At school, we were just starting to study the earth's history. I shook my head.

"Well," Al continued, looking back into the dark pool. "It's interesting to think about."

"Yes," I agreed." I wanted to learn more about snapping turtles. I stared into the darkness of the deep pool and made another silent promise to myself.

Nineteen

SLASH & TWITCH

Alton pushed open the door of greenhouse No. 3. "Good morning."

"Morning, Al. You're here early," Rachel replied.

"Yes. I hoped to speak to you while Sam is still doing his chores."

Rachel sat back on her heels and looked up at him.

Alton waved a hand at her. "Everything is great. Sam and I've been talking about shelter building lately. He did a fine job on some of the little shelters he made in the clearing last spring, and he's been asking a lot about log cabins."

"I think I know why," Rachel said.

"I thought I'd offer to help. I've built several in my lifetime. Just little ones. One for Alice and me when we were young, which we used as a fishing camp, and a couple bigger cabins for some friends over the years."

"I didn't know that, but I know *you,* Al, and I'm betting you've thought this through."

"Probably not enough," Al replied with a laugh. He gestured toward the creek. "I have cruised the woods near the big clearing both upstream and down. I think for a nice little cabin with a small loft, we'd need about fifty logs. Just upstream from the clearing is a nice stand of spruce and fir that look like they were harvested about fifty or so years ago. There's an old skidder trail right through the middle of it. I think it'd be pretty easy to haul the logs out to the clearing by hand. Hauling them by hand or with come-alongs would mean the biggest trees we could harvest would be about eleven or twelve inches in the butt section and only about fourteen feet long. Sam and I should be able to manage that size, all right. Once dried, the logs wouldn't be too heavy for us to roll up some purlins into place on the cabin walls. I think it's very doable."

Rachel smiled up at Alton. "I knew you'd have thought it through. Though I think Sam is too young to operate a chainsaw."

"Of course, that's your call. I can do all the chainsaw work; Sam can help with everything else. If we don't hurry our work, everything will be very safe. I will teach him that. There'll be many things for him to do: peeling bark, boring holes for the spikes, preparing the quarter rounds, tamping in the oakum, and such."

"Alton, I think it would be a great experience for him. I also think Teri will want to help if that'd be okay with you. Come fall, maybe I can help a little too."

"That would be wonderful," replied Al.

"As I said, I've inspected the tree stands, but if you'd like to walk them with me, I'd know which trees you'd like me to harvest."

"No, I'm afraid I have too much to do on the farm at this time of year. I trust you, and to be honest, I don't really care which trees. Not if it's just spruce or fir."

"All right then. I will select and mark the trees and not cut them too close together. Sam and I will also trim all of the treetops and haul them to the edge of the old skidder trail. Next fall, we'll cut them stove-length. They're softwood, but they'll make decent firewood, especially for kindling."

"Excellent. We can never have too much firewood."

"Agreed. I think Sam will enjoy the build."

With that, Alton offered to help with any pressing farm chores. When Rachel declined the offer, Al left for home.

The prospect of building another small log cabin lifted Alton and made him feel ten years younger. There was much to do, and the first was to have his chainsaw serviced and for him to sharpen it. His summer just got a lot better.

The next afternoon, as Alton and I approached the creek, Al stood with both hands on his hips and surveyed the clearing near my Adirondack shelter. He looked up into the treetops and made some notes in his little book. He looked up the creek and then down it. He pulled an old compass from his pocket, flipped it open, and regarded it.

Still looking at the compass face, he turned his body deliberately toward the creek and faced a little bit downstream.

"That's south," he said. "That's how we want to orient it."

"Orient what?" I asked.

"I spoke to your Mother yesterday while you were watering the hanging baskets. We discussed it for quite a while, and she thinks it would be a good idea if we built a cabin here."

"Really?" I shouted.

Al smiled down at me. "We have her permission."

Our own cabin! I wondered if Mom mentioned to him that she and my Dad had talked about building one years ago. I still felt bad for telling him myself.

Al flipped a page in his notebook. "First thing we'll have to do is some serious planning. Let's start with the land."

We sat down on the same log that my Mom and I had sat on while making s'mores a week earlier. With the notebook in his lap, Alton drew a perfect outline of the clearing and the winding creek. Then he drew four points of the compass on the borders of the page.

"North, South, East, and West – these are the cardinal points of the compass. We want to orient the cabin so that the front, with most of the windows, is facing south. That way, we'll be able to get the majority of the day's sunlight." Then, he drew a rectangle on the page.

"What do you think about this?" he asked.

"I don't know much about this stuff," I said, "but I can imagine it — it looks good."

We put the rectangle about fifty feet from the creek.

"I oriented the cabin a little bit south-southeast, so that will also get a little of the morning sun."

We spent the rest of the afternoon picking up sticks and cleaning the clearing of stumps and loose rocks. When it was time to go home, Alton said, "When you're finished with your chores tomorrow, meet me in the barn."

I must've looked excited to start our cabin because he followed with, "But don't hurry your work. Do every job the best you can; I'm sure you know by now if you're watering and miss a hanging basket or a flat of seedlings, they can die, lickety-split."

"Yes, sir," I said. "I learned that the hard way."

"Attaboy."

⁂

The next day, I found Al in the barn, bent over the big, heavy vice that was bolted to the workbench. There was a propane torch on the bench and a short-handled sledgehammer.

"There," he said, unwinding the vice's handle, "a log dog."

"A log … *dog*?" He held up a piece of round iron about two feet long; four inches at both ends were bent ninety-degrees in the same direction with sharpened ends.

"Yessir. As we notch the log ends, we'll need something to secure them, to hold them still and steady. These will do it." He tossed the newly bent log dog onto the bench with four others. Laid out on the bench also were the sledgehammer and regular carpenter's hammer, a big gouge, an equally larger wood chisel, the small hand axe, a metal file, a heavy six-inch long bolt, and a vice grip. At the end of the row of tools were things I didn't know the name of. Alton saw me pondering them.

"These," he said, picking up one of the odd-looking tools, "are what we use to peel the bark off the logs. This is called a draw knife, and these things are called peeling spuds. This is called a scribe, or a pencil compass, which we'll use to mark and notch the logs. You'll learn all about these once the trees are down and the logs are yarded to the building site."

Just then, Teri breezed into the barn.

"Howdy, boys!"

"Morning, Teri."

"I heard you two are going to build a cabin." She hugged Al with one arm and then leaned down and kissed the top of my head. Al smiled broadly.

She continued, "When it comes time to peel the logs, I'll be there to help. I did it one summer when I had a camp counselor job in high school, and I really liked it. Something about it was really—appealing."

"Oh, good one!" Al laughed. "You work on that all morning?"

"Pretty much. When will you start felling trees?"

"Probably tomorrow or the day after," Alton said. "We have to clear an old skidder trail enough that we can haul the logs out."

"I can help out on the weekend," Teri replied. "Do you plan on harvesting then?"

"You bet," Al said.

"I'll bring some gloves. In the morning, I'm going to help Rachel move some plants between greenhouses, and then I'll find you two. It'll do me good. I've been getting soft lately, anyway." Teri winked at me.

Teri? Getting soft? Since I could remember, she had always been nothing but red hair, green eyes, and muscle. She was tough and had a reputation for standing on her own and not suffering fools. Mom always said that about her.

Just like Alton had said, the next day we started clearing a path from the cabin site next to the creek upstream into the big stand of spruce and fir trees.

"This is going to be some of the toughest work," he told me. "I'm glad you brought some heavy gloves. I'll start cutting saplings and brush, and you can follow behind and toss all the leavings into small brush piles off to the side. It'll be helpful if you make the piles about ten feet apart. That way, we'll have room to twitch the logs out onto the path without tripping over lots of slash. We'll go slow … the most important thing is safety."

He looked at me. "Any questions?"

"Just one," I said. "What's a twitch, and what's a slash?"

"Oh, yes. A twitch is what the old-timers called a log, or several logs, that are ready to be hauled out of the woods and off to the sawmills. But it's also a verb; we'll twitch the logs to the cabin. Guess that means I'm officially an old-timer. Once we get the trees down, we'll first have to cut all the branches off the logs. Slash is a term for all the twigs and branches that are too small to be cut into firewood … sticks too small to be of any use."

We worked for four hours before taking a lunch break at the cabin site. Alton used his chainsaw, a hatchet, a larger double-bit axe, and what he called a surveyor's axe, which had an axe handle but a very thin, sharp blade on the end—like a knife blade. It was very hard work, almost as hard as pulling the plastic mulch out of the fields in the autumn. I winced as I stretched my back and clenched my aching hands into fists. After we finished our break, we did it for three more hours. We carried out all the tools to the wagon that we'd left in the clearing, and once there, we turned around. Al didn't say anything at first as we looked down what now appeared to be a road into the woods.

Then he patted me on my sweat-soaked shoulder. "Strong work."

I just nodded and said, "What's next?"

"Day after tomorrow," he replied, "we'll pick out fifty trees and knock 'em down."

I managed a tired smile. My shoulders screamed, and the tendons in my hands and back throbbed, but I couldn't wait to work the woods again.

Twenty
WE GO LOGGING

We loaded the little red wagon with as much gear as it would hold: axes, ropes, gloves, our lunches, and a big-handled contraption with cables, a lever with a handle on it, and metal hooks on both ends of the cables. Alton saw me looking it over.

"That's called a come-along. Ever seen one before?"

I shook my head. "Looks cool, though."

"Yes," Al said. "It is cool, I suppose. It will move objects that are far too heavy for us to budge." Al pointed at the tool. "When we crank the handle, it will pull a downed, limbed log along the ground. That's how we'll twitch the logs out to the trail we made. Once we get at least forty-eight good logs out alongside the trail, I think we can get that old Ford tractor down there and pull them to the building site. Then the real work begins!"

Alton saw me raise my eyebrows and slapped me on the back.

"It'll be fun and worth the work. Trust me."

I did trust Alton as much as a person can trust anybody. But the next few days that we worked in the woods was as hard as anything I'd ever done. Harder than any of my farm chores. It might've been because, as Al suggested, I was using different muscles than normal. Al marked all the trees he wanted to cut down. One by one we felled the trees, limbed them, and dragged them to the cabin site. It took five days. On the first day, Alton explained how to cut the trees to make them fall (hopefully) in the direction he wanted them to land, and he preached about safety over and over with each tree. Every time he got ready to start the chainsaw, he first had me come over to the base of the tree and he carefully taught me how to notch the tree. Then, he sent me standing far off in the distance, telling me where to stand for each tree.

Once a tree slammed to the ground, he limbed it, cutting off the branches flush with the tree bark. Sometimes, he'd walk along the top of the fallen log with the chainsaw going, cutting off the remaining branches. It was a wonder to see this seventy-something-old man walking on a log like it was a balance beam. *With* a running chainsaw. Once it was limbed, Al used a tape measure and cut the log to make it twenty feet long. He would wave me over, and together we would clear the slash enough so we could walk alongside the log and pull it out with the come-along.

Fifty times we repeated the process. By Saturday afternoon, all the logs were at the building site, stacked neatly into four piles. As we got ready to quit for the day, Alton and I sat on one of the logs, looking at all we had accomplished.

"That was the hard part," he said. "now we peel the bark off. That's not hard to do; it's just tedious. But we'll get started in a couple of days after my old bones get a rest. Next Sunday, your Mom and Teri will help us finish what logs are left. Building the cabin is the fun part. It won't even seem like work at all."

Alton pushed my baseball cap back on my head and patted my shoulder. "You did a good job helping with the logs."

I smiled up at him.

I saw him looking at my brand-new and now tattered gloves. "When we were using the come-along, and you were placing those short segments of branches under them, so they rolled along the forest floor—that was helpful."

"Yeah," I said. "On the third day, it sorta felt like we were never going to get all the logs we needed."

I looked around at the four piles of logs. I could imagine each one, the bark peeled and golden colored, being lifted onto the walls of the cabin.

"I feel like we've accomplished a lot already."

Al grunted as he stood up from the log. "Before we go, grab me four stout sticks, about two feet long, would you?"

I did so as Al used his tape measure and measured the ground diagonally. Using the back of an axe, he drove the sticks into the soil. He measured several times, pulling the stakes and adjusting them. He took a spool of baling twine and strung the string all the way around the stakes. He stood inside the square and turned toward the creek and pointed both index fingers at the creek.

"Well," he said, "I think this looks good. I'll re-measure when we come back, but I think this will be the footprint of the cabin … right here."

I could see it. It wasn't hard to imagine a little cabin with smoke rising from a chimney. I had a big grin on my face, and he did too.

When Alton did return, he was moving a little slower and stiffer, but he was eager to get to work. We loaded the wagon with a few draw knives, a file, the small hatchet, two log dogs, and a tool Al called a peeling spud.

The cabin site now looked like a construction site. The babbling creek looked the same, but the four piles of logs and the worn-down paths from the little tractor had transformed the clearing. Al walked a short way down the path from where we'd cut the trees and, from one of the slash piles, he cut six three-foot sections of heavy branches. We carried them back to the building site, and he tied two tripods together to use as make-shift sawhorses. We picked up a stacked log one end at a time and set them on the tripods.

"Now," he said, "the peeling begins."

Using a draw knife, Al showed me how to walk along the length of the log, drawing the blade toward him, taking long strips of bark off. The strip of bark flipped off the log onto the ground. Where there had been no branches, the strips were two to three feet long. Then, he picked up the peeling spud and worked the short blade under the edge of the bark. He used the spud to pry big sheets of bark off the log. It took about thirty minutes to peel the entire log. Then, we plopped it onto the ground and rolled it about fifteen feet away. The newly peeled log was pretty and almost golden in the early morning light.

"Not too bad," Alton said. "Forty-nine to go."

I squinted up at him, and he winked at me. He stepped up to the pile and reached for the next log. We repeated the process. After seven logs, I got pretty good at using the drawknife. I learned that the spruce trees were easier to peel than the fir and that if there is a knot where a branch had been, the bark peeled easier if you first knocked the knot off with the hatchet.

After the eighth log, Al looked at his watch. "We've been at it for over four hours. Let's take a break."

We both found a comfortable spot to sit facing the creek and drank some water.

While we rested, Alton's lessons began again. Something flitted in the air in front of us.

"Oh, are we going to have a little hatch?" he asked.

I glanced first at him, then in the direction of his gaze, and saw an insect fly by. Alton quickly jumped up and, in a single motion, removed his hat and scooped the fly into it. It was a mayfly.

"Ah," Al said. "A Hendrickson. Getting late in the spring for these guys." He handed me his hat, and I looked at the delicate mayfly clinging to the fabric.

"You know," he said, "In some eastern streams and rivers—like in Pennsylvania and New York—the emergence of these Hendricksons are highly anticipated. It's usually the first major hatch of the season in certain streams. Fly fishers wait all winter for them to hatch."

"I've seen them before," I said. "I'm never sure which kind of fly I'm looking at when I see them, but I'm sure I've seen this very kind before." I studied the little bug closely. "But, come to think of it, the colors were different. They might've been a different mayfly after all."

"Possibly," Al replied, "you might've seen these; the color varies quite a bit in different environments—even within the same creek or stream. Do you remember when we talked about the mayflies more than a month ago?"

"Yes, you said the ugly larvae of the mayflies live underwater for a year or so, but when they come to the surface, they only live a short time.

Oh—and when the mayflies dip their tails into the water they're dropping eggs."

"Very good," Al replied. "The more you can read about the different insects the trout and salmon feed on, the better equipped you'll be as a fly fisherman. But that doesn't mean you have to memorize everything about them."

I nodded as I looked closer at the Hendrickson still clinging to the inside of his hat.

I could feel Al look at me.

"Sam, do you think you read slowly because you want to understand what you're reading better, or do you feel you don't see the words well? It's none of my business, I'm just curious. I think I read slowly also."

"Mom says my eyesight is as good as Ted Williams's. He was a baseball player. I guess he had good eyes. Anyways, I don't need glasses. I got checked by a doctor."

Alton too looked closely at the delicate little Hendrickson mayfly. "You should see what these look like under a microscope."

"That would be so cool," I said.

We went back to work and peeled three more logs before quitting for the day. Pulling the wagon back to the barn, Al said, "With a little help, we might have them all peeled by the end of the weekend. Then, we re-stack them carefully so they'll dry-out all summer. Come fall, we'll put up the walls.

"I can't wait."

Al laughed. "We'll have to; we can't start the walls if the logs aren't dried-out. In the old days, homesteaders timed things so that the logs sat drying all summer and winter. Then, they'd start building the cabins in the spring … and move in in the fall. But in my experience, if they dry all summer, and if we stack them so the air can circulate around them, they'll be ready this fall."

"Okay," I said.

Before he got into his Jeep, he gave me a high five. Good work today, Sam."

Then he said, "Yeah, Ted Williams had pretty sharp eyes."

Twenty-one

WE PROCEED

I was still watering plants when Alton arrived the next morning. He drove into the driveway pulling a small trailer filled with a dozen very large tree stumps and a bunch of new tools. Each wooden tree stump was about a foot and a half in length and bigger than that in diameter.

As I walked up to his Jeep, Al jumped out and said, "These, my boy, are what the cabin is going to sit on. They're cedar, so they won't rot for many, many years. I traded for them with a friend of mine who has a cedar mill."

We switched the trailer from his Jeep to the old Ford tractor and hauled them to the cabin site. Alton made many more measurements with his tape measure and the string before committing to where each cedar stump would be placed.

"These measurements are temporary—I just want an idea of the footprint. Do you know what the footprint is?" he asked.

"The mark your shoe makes in the mud?"

"When building a cabin, it's the outline of where it will sit. It's important. The corners of the footprint also have to be perfectly square. How easily the roof goes on later depends on this."

Once the stumps were in place, we returned to peeling logs.

"Our goal," he said, "will be ten logs a day. That'll be a fair amount of work."

And we met our goal. It was very hard work, but we did it. At the end of the day, we used an old rake from the barn and swept all the peelings of bark into a huge pile about twenty feet from the creek. On the third day, we repeated the process, but only got eight logs peeled. I could hardly straighten my back, and I think Alton was getting sore and a little worn out too.

"Tomorrow is Friday," Al said, "I think we'll take it off and rest. We'll fish if you want to on Saturday and finish the last bunch of logs on Sunday. Then we will let the sun do its job."

"Sounds good to me," I said. My arms were so sore on Friday I didn't even fish.

Saturday morning Alton called the house and told Mother he wasn't going to fish. He needed one more day to rest. He and Mother talked for a while on the phone.

"Is Al coming today?" I asked.

"No, Honey," she said. "I think he's still a little tired and sore from all the logging work this week. You know, Sam, Alton is in his seventies. I hope he doesn't push himself too hard."

I looked at my oatmeal. I hadn't thought of that. "Me too," I said, and I began to worry.

"He's coming early tomorrow morning," Mother said. "He and Teri will join us for breakfast and then we'll all go down to the creek and try to finish peeling the last logs. You and I will get up extra early and water all the greenhouses before they get here."

"Okay."

After chores, I spent the rest of the day looking at books about insects. I went to the creek but didn't see any mayflies, though there were several caddis flies flitting around the streambanks. I knew they were caddis flies because unlike mayflies, which normally fly in more or less straight lines, caddis flies fly willy-nilly. Alton said, "Like tiny helicopters whose navigational systems were down and they were trying to avoid a bad landing."

The next morning, I had finished watering and was helping Mother stir the breakfast home fries when Alton and Teri arrived. Teri gave Al a big hug in the driveway before they entered the kitchen. His eyes were bright, and he had a bounce to his step.

"Did you fish, Sam?" he asked as he flipped his hat onto a hook by the door.

"No, but I walked the creek and tried to study some mayflies." Al nodded his approval.

"I only saw caddis flies," I said. "They were trying not to crash land."

Teri gave me a funny look, but Al winked at me and smiled. I was glad he looked rested. When we arrived at the creek after breakfast, Mother and Teri stared at the building site. It was clean, and the clearing was much more open. It almost resembled a yard.

"Wow," Mother said. "I knew you put in the time last week, but I had no idea you'd come this far along."

"Great work," Teri offered. She walked to the edge of the path we'd cut into the stands of spruce and fir. It looked like a road now. She looked at the ground. "You got the old tractor in here."

"Yes," replied Alton. "It took some doing, but we did it."

We had fun working together. I hoped Mother was impressed by how I had learned how to work the logs safely, and I truly felt that in only a week, I had gotten stronger. I was certainly more confident. I showed Mother how to use the log dogs to secure the logs so they wouldn't roll around while you peeled them.

In only five hours, the four of us peeled all the bark off the remaining logs and stacked them. There were four piles of logs again. But now they were, to me at least, beautiful. They were a pretty golden brown, and the most recently peeled logs were glistening wet from the sap and sparkled in the midday sun.

"There's a formula for stacking logs," Al said, "for the proper amount of space between the logs for air circulation. There should be enough room for a mouse to run between them, but not enough room for the cat chasing it."

"If we do this part well," Al said, "they might dry out enough this summer, and we won't have to wait until spring to throw up the cabin."

Throw up the cabin, I thought. *Sounds easy enough. Al had said that will be the fun part.*

Occasionally, Al had to start the chainsaw to knock down a stubborn knot that was too big for the little hatchet. If we didn't knock them flat where they stick out from the logs, peeling was difficult. At one point, Alton called to me as he was adding gasoline to the saw.

"Sam, what do my notes say over there about the gas/oil mixture?"

I picked up the piece of paper near his jacket and started carrying it to him.

"No," he said. "I don't have my reading glasses. Can you just read it to me, please?"

I didn't want to. It might take too long. But it was awkward. Mother and Teri just ignored what we were talking about and kept working.

So, I did. "*Ra- Re- Re-mem-* Remember to *Ma- mii- Mick-* Mix *oh-ole-* oil, … I finally had it. "Remember to mix the oil 40:1." (Only I pronounced it, "Forty-*two dots*-one.")

Neither Mother nor Teri looked up but Teri was smiling.

"Thanks, Partner," Al said. "I don't think I've mentioned it, but my eyes are failing me these days."

"Oh," I said. "I'm sorry."

Al waved his hand in the air. "Ah … It's just part of getting old. The worst part is I had to buy special glasses just to be able to tie flies onto my line."

When we were finished, we all found rocks or stumps to sit on and ate some of Mother's cold fried chicken. The sun had been out from behind the clouds for a couple of hours, so Mother started getting antsy.

Halfway through lunch, she jumped up and said, "I'd better water the greenhouses. Are you guys all right to bring back the tools?"

"I'll help water," Teri announced and stood up.

Al spoke up. "There are four houses. Why don't we each take a house since it's getting hot?"

"Oh, that'd be great," Mother replied, and we packed up quickly and headed back to the farm.

Twenty-two
I Get to Help Alton

The rest of the summer was spent fishing and practicing casting the fly rod. Alton came by the farm two or three times a week to help with the farm chores. He seemed to like the work a lot. Every Sunday, Mom invited Alton for supper, and most weeks, he accepted. Teri was always there anyway, and the four of us had fun discussing farming, fishing, the news from that week. Everyone seemed sick of the war in Vietnam, which was why we never watched TV during suppertime, and once Teri started crying when they were talking about it.

On the Fourth of July, the four of us piled into mother's old Suburban, the only road-legal vehicle we had on the farm and drove into Milton to watch the fireworks the townspeople shot over the big river. Afterward, we went for ice cream cones.

One evening after supper, Mom came to my room and asked if I had been reading enough. She wanted me to try to read every day during the summer. She said that's the only way I'd improve. I had been reading, I told her, but I wasn't getting any faster.

"Alton came to me yesterday and asked if I thought you'd mind reading to him a few times a week. His eyes are failing, Sam, and I think it would be a nice thing to do."

"Mom, you know I couldn't! Can't you or Teri do it?"

She looked seriously at me. "Exactly when are my chores finished on the farm?" she asked. "I'm still working on things long after you've gone to bed, you know."

And I did know that. She never stopped working.

"And Teri has her own life, even though we'd rather she lived here with us. She almost does, come to think of it. But she's busy too. You can do it, Sam. It's the least we can do for that lovely man, for all he's done for us … for all he has taught you."

"I know," I said, bowing my head. "It's just … my reading …"

"Honey, Al was a teacher for decades. Maybe this could be a good thing for both of you. He'll get his novels finished, at least by listening to them, and you'll most likely improve your reading. You are always trying to learn something, are you not?"

"I love learning new things."

"Well, at least try it this week. If it's too uncomfortable for you, I'll say you can stop. Deal?"

"Okay," I said. "I'll try."

"You know I think you're the best boy ever, right?" She kissed me on the head.

Alton showed up the very next day in the early afternoon. *Oh, God,* I thought. *Now I have to read to him.*

"Hi, Sammy Boy," he said as he stepped from the Jeep. "Are you free for the rest of the day?"

"All my chores are done," I said.

"Want to go fishing?"

I was relieved. "Sure! I'll check with Mom."

We secured permission to fish for the rest of the day. Not only that, I was with Alton, so that meant we could fish whichever section of the creek we wanted.

We walked far upstream from the big maples to the quick water. As we walked, I noticed that I looked at the forest differently now. I'd see a tall, straight spruce tree or a fir and think, *That one would make a good cabin log*, or, *That one has too many branches and would be a tough one to peel.* I also thought about how the spruce bark would peel much easier than the fir trees.

When we got to a nice pool, we stopped. Here the trees had not been harvested for generations, and the creek was darkened by the towering spruces and thick cedars, their shadows and reflections stretching out across the water, and the dark water was broken only by ripples around boulders or from the silvery circles made by tiny rising fish.

Both of us put our sections of fly rods together and strung the line through the guides. "Rigging up," we called it. I was careful not to miss any guides. While I rigged my rod, I tried to watch the creek for rising fish. Only one set of ripples I thought might've been made by a slightly bigger fish than the rises we had seen made by the little parr or chubs. I opened my fly box to choose a fly, but Al said, "Let's give it a moment. Part of the fun is figuring out what fly to use, and we're in no hurry." Al reached up and gently shook a cedar bough. A few flittering flies flew off in different directions.

"Caddis flies," I said. "Probably Zebra Caddis."

Al smiled at me.

"What? Am I way off?"

"No," he replied. "You're correct. But look what you've learned already this year: you can identify mayflies versus caddis flies by their flight, you cast really well already, you know how to yard logs and how to peel the bark, you can build usable shelters. You're coming along far—and fast."

"It doesn't feel far. When I watch you work on things, I feel I have so far to go."

Al laughed. "Well now, I've been at things for over seventy years, and when I watch you do things, it *feels* like ninety years. I can't move like I used to."

Just then we both heard a little "*glub*" sound from the creek and we looked up to see some bigger rings on the surface.

"I bet that was a trout," Al whispered. "What size do you think those caddis were?"

"Maybe a size eighteen," I whispered back.

"Why don't you tie on a small elk hair caddis."

I nodded and retrieved one from my box and tied it to the tippet of my leader with a clinch knot.

"You want to go first?" I asked.

"No, sir. You go right ahead." He squinted to tie his fly on.

I payed out a little fly line and, raising the rod to overhead, dropped it in line with the head of the pool, upstream from where we saw the fish rise. The fly settled onto the surface in a good spot, and I gently stripped in any slack line. I kept the rod tip pointed toward the fly and followed it as it drifted into the deeper part of the pool. I was surprised how quickly the fish attacked the fly. There was a violent splash and the fly was gone! Instinctively, I gently raised the rod tip and had him hooked. The line went taut and the bend in the rod tip sent the message to my hand that it was a bigger fish than I was used to. The line darted left and then moved in hurried circles in the dark water, and when we saw the fish flash just under the surface, we knew it was a trout, and a big one for Dibbin Creek.

"Don't horse him!" Alton exclaimed. I tried to loosen the grip I had on the fly line in case the fish wanted to take a little.

I quickly became worried that I would lose the trout, so I started backing up into the fern and alders. One step backward, a second step … then on the third I lifted the trout onto the mossy bank. Alton knelt by the pool, wetted his hand in the water, and grabbed the trout. He effortlessly removed the fly from the corner of the trout's mouth and with a big grin he held it up to show me.

"Thirteen inches for sure," he said, "good fish for this water."

I looked closely at the beautiful colors on the dark fish: the yellow and red spots with the faint blue halos around them, and the lighter worm-like lines against the darker hue of brown on its back and fins. It was the biggest fish I'd ever caught, including chubs.

"Let's get him back in the water," Al said.

Before I could speak, before I could respond, Alton reached down and suspended the beautiful fish just under the surface of the pool. He held his hand open, cradling the fish's belly, careful not to grip the animal. I still couldn't speak. I couldn't say that I might want to take the trout home to show Mom, nor did I have time to suggest she might want to eat it. Because before I could, the fish slowly swam into the depths of the pool.

I do not know what look I had on my face. Alton watched the trout swim and, still kneeling, he turned to me, still smiling. "That was beautiful. You casted, hooked him, and played him beautifully, Sam."

That did make me feel better, but I may have looked a bit stunned.

Alton squinted up at me. "I should've asked if I could release it. I'm sorry, Sam, it's simply automatic for me these days. You see, a fish like that, it's at the top of the genetic pyramid in a creek this size. He probably has two or three years of spawning left in him. If we want to preserve the trout population, most of what we catch here we should release. Especially these big, strong guys."

How could I be disappointed? It made perfect sense.

We continued to fish for a couple of hours, each of us catching several more trout in the five-to-seven inch range. After we fished our way down to the slower water by the big maples and started catching chubs again, we found an old log to sit on and broke down our rods. It was a great day.

Alton spoke up. "I hope you don't mind me letting your big trout go. I should have asked."

"No," I said. "I get it."

He looked up at the cedars that leaned out over the creek. "You know, as I get older, conservation, not just conserving fish, but of all nature, has become more important to me. I suppose that's probably normal. But, sometimes, I get sad and I think conservation as only a delaying action. I worry about the future; I think there are too many people on the planet. I think population growth is a relentless, unavoidable threat to the preservation of our lands. And people are becoming indifferent to the natural environment. Add to that the increasing population means greater demands upon our resources for power, more homes, roads, lumber, and so on." Al looked sad. "Folks seem more content with televisions, motels, telephones, and fancy motorboats. Flyfishing is different. It's one sport wherein the essence of the pursuit and catch of the quarry can be done without damaging the environment."

Al lost me again with some of what he was saying, but I wanted to keep the conversation rolling, so I asked, "How do we fix it, this conservation thing?"

Alton sighed and shook his head. "Vote, when you're old enough.

And volunteer in any way you can." He stared up into the cedars again. "Who will preserve the land and the rivers? I suppose the government, God forbid. It will eventually come down to an appraisal of values, but who will do the appraising?" Al tossed a tiny twig into the creek and watched it float. "The *majority* will, I reckon. But that's what worries me; already the majority do not even know about the natural world, much less regard it as something precious . . . something priceless that, once lost, will be lost forever. And in a few years, when I'm gone, there will be one less voice for conservation. I think developers will always want to keep putting up hotels and parking lots."

I was still struggling to follow some of what he was talking about, but I realized I better figure it out, and fast, because Al reached over, mussed up my hair, and said, "It'll be youngsters like you who'll have to grow up and stop 'em."

It sounded serious. I straightened my back. My eyes focused in on him. I was going to vote someday, whatever that was, and I was going to vote for the fish! You could bet on it.

Al must've sensed my acceptance of the awesome responsibility. "Don't worry about it now. My advice for all people your age is to read, read, and read some more. The more self-educated you become the better off you'll be. And you're already a flyfisher. You can be proud of that."

That, I understood. I faintly smiled and stood up tall and straight.

Twenty-three
MOTHER AND ALTON HATCH A PLAN

I spent a good deal of the rest of the summer learning all that I could about insects and artificial flies. And a few days each week I spent on the porch, reading to Alton. I didn't understand why he couldn't just wear the fancy reading glasses that he used to tie flies onto his very fine leader. He said it had to do with distance. The first novel he wanted to listen to was *Call of the Wild* by Jack London. I had never tried to read many of the classic books, but when I turned thirteen on July 9th, Alton told Mother it was "High time he does."

The reading sessions started out rough.

We sat close to each other in the rocking chairs. I held the old book, and Alton took out the small notebook he always had in his shirt pocket.

He was always drawing sketches or taking notes of things to look up later and read about.

I held the book in my lap, but we sat talking for the first few minutes.

Alton sniffed the late summer afternoon air. "You can smell the Perry's fields from here. They're spreading manure already."

"I actually don't mind it," I said.

"Mind it? I *like* it. My wife Alice thought I was crazy, but I enjoy the smell of cow manure on a field. It's comforting, somehow."

"What was Alice like?"

Al smiled. "You're stalling. I'll tell you about her another time. Let's start this novel."

I opened the book. My hands were shaking.

"Skip the poem at the beginning," Al said. "It's just London trying to be fancy."

I nodded.

"Buc—Buck did not ree—read the nee, now—newpap—" I looked up at Al, hoping he would read the word for me. He didn't. "*Nowspaper*?"

"Good," he said softly. But plural. He pointed at the word. "The 'ew' is pronounced 'oooh.' NEWspaper—see?"

I nodded. "That makes sense." I kept trying and got hung up again in the first sentence.

Alton watched me trace my index finger along the bottom of the text. I always do that. He did not want to say the word for me, knowing that that's probably what my mother and teachers did for me, but he had a trick. He covered the 'ing' in brewing and said, "Remember the 'ew' sound you just learned?"

I got it immediately. "Brew!"

"That's it." Then, he removed his finger.

"Brewing." I said, shaking my head. It was easier the way he was teaching me.

"*Brewing*. That's not a simple word, so don't be discouraged. Keep going."

"...not al—al—alone for him—himsal—himsalf." I stopped reading and shook my head.

"It's fine, Sam, just fine. It's not a race against a clock. We'll take the time you need."

I squinted at him. This was another one of those times when I had no idea what Al was talking about, but he often seemed to get a kick out of the things he said. I continued but couldn't figure out the words 'tide-water.'

Alton put his hand on my forearm, and I stopped. I couldn't even get the first sentence out. "Try not to get frustrated. It's just reading, and reading can be improved. Let me ask you something. I know you say you read slowly. But do you *like* to read?"

"Sure," I replied. "I like books, but sometimes they don't seem to like me. Not sure if that makes sense." I thought for a moment to try to explain, and Al gave me time. "I love finding out the things books tell me, but sometimes I get so frustrated trying to read, I don't get anything from them. I end up skipping whole sections of the book—even when I'm excited about the topic. Unless there are pictures. If there are lots of pictures, I can usually make sense of things."

Al nodded. "Okay, let's try an experiment." Al opened his notebook and wrote something. Then he said, "Close the book for a minute." I did as the old man said.

Al wrote on several pages, two letters on each page. He held his thumb over one letter at a time and asked me to tell him the sound of the exposed one.

"C," I said, "Either '*See*,' or '*Ka*.'"

"Good. And this one?"

"F." Then I made a '*Fffpft*' sound.

"One more," Al said.

"V. Like Vvffft."

Alton nodded. "I want you to try something. Press all four of your fingers gently over the front of your throat like this." I felt my throat. "Good. Now leave them there and sound out the 'V' for me. Just the letter Vvvv…"

I did as he asked.

"Can you feel a vibration in your fingertips?"

"Yes."

"Okay. Leave your fingers there and now say the 'F.'"

I made the sound. "Hmm, that's different. No vibration."

"Do adults try to help you read by finishing words and sentences for you?"

"All the time. It makes it easier. But sometimes there's nobody around."

"Exactly," Al responded. "You just said two things that are interesting, 'the adults make it easier,' and 'sometimes no one is around.' I think it might not be helpful for people to finish words and sentences for you, and it would be helpful for you to get better at reading when you're alone. What do you think?"

I shrugged my shoulders. I couldn't tell if I was lazy, in trouble for not trying enough, or just plain dumb. "I think I should try a lot harder?"

Alton smiled but also looked sad. "Sam, you try plenty hard. I have some thoughts, but I think your mom should hear them. Are you up for that?"

Before I could answer, he said, "Don't worry … it's just some ideas I have that might help you along a bit. But I'll have to talk to your mom first."

I felt embarrassed, which I knew I would. Al probably thought I was "slow," like Will Mooney always said at school. I hated Will Mooney, but not Al. I wanted him, more than anyone, to like me.

"Why don't you work on the first couple of pages while I go talk to her."

I nodded, and Al got up and called into the kitchen. "Rachel, are you in a place where you can talk for a minute?"

"Of course," she said.

Al looked out the window and saw Sam staring at the book. Then he sat in a kitchen chair. "I fear I'm about to overstep my bounds in a big way."

"Oh?"

"I've suspected for some time that Sam might be dyslexic."

Rachel snapped a quick look at Alton.

"It's really none of my business," Al quickly offered, "and I won't speak more of it if that's what you want."

"No, we can talk about it. I've suspected something was going on for a long time, but the teachers haven't mentioned anything. Except, I have heard a few mentions in the past couple of years that he's a smart boy, and eloquent when speaking, but when he has to read aloud in class, he gets annoyed. Sometimes at school, he complains of abdominal pains or headaches and has to visit the school nurse. They never find anything wrong with him. One teacher put it together and it seems to coincide with reading assignments."

Alton smiled and nodded.

"Al, I have tried to help him with his reading a lot, as much as time allows, I promise you."

"Oh, I know Rachel. That's precisely why I bring it up. You know I was a teacher, not the right kind of teacher to tutor reading, but I have the time. I think maybe I could help him this summer."

Rachel reached for Al's forearm and then let go. "You would do that? Tutor Sam?"

"Certainly. I'd have to bone up on dyslexia, but at worst, I don't think it would hurt at all. Do you think Sam will go along with it?"

"Oh, I think so, if it's you."

"I suspect kids with reading disabilities need structure, a set schedule. But, at first, I think I'd like to read together in an unstructured way. Make it incidental, like looking up fish, insects, trees, and other things he's interested in so it might feel less like tutoring to him."

Rachel sat staring at Al with her elbow on her thigh and her chin in her hand. "You know, Al, a year ago, Sam seemed more disconnected. He lost track of time easily, he often seemed lost in daydreams, and some days he would come home from school sad or angry. He lacked self-esteem. Teri and I saw it, and it broke our hearts. Once, he got off the bus and was feeling down. When I asked him if something happened at school, he said no, but then asked me if he was stupid. He asked me to be honest. Stupid is a word I never use. All I could do was hold him and tell him, 'No, no, no,' and how proud I was of him. I asked questions to find where that was coming from, but he insisted there was no bullying at school."

Rachel's eyes watered. "But now, he is fly fishing already. He seems excited every day about the things you teach him and tries to study up on things on his own even more than he used to. And now, you're going to help him become a reader. Al, I'm starting to wonder if you're not a godsend."

"Oh, hardly. But he is a good boy. I like that he tries so hard and never complains about the farm chores. And I like how much he loves you and Teri.

"Where is Teri, by the way? I haven't seen her here for nearly a week?"

"She is at an artist's retreat out on the coast. She'll be back tomorrow."

"I see. All right then." Al pushed himself up from the chair. "I'll go work with Sam a little bit now."

"Thank you Al … very much."

He smiled at her.

"I want you to know, Al, that Teri was right—you are part of this farm family. What'd she call us? 'Weird?' From now on, I will make every night's table setting for four, I already routinely set one for Teri, and any night you aren't with us, I'll just put the plate away after supper. But there'll always be a place for you."

On his way to the door, Al turned to tell her that wouldn't be necessary, but her face told him it was best not to say it. So again, he smiled at her. Then he nodded and went back onto the porch.

Rachel went to the kitchen window that looks onto the porch. She watched Al settle into the rocker and lean over Sam to see what page he was on. Then she saw Al reach down and point at something in the book, and Sam look up at Al, and both man and boy laughed. She could see all that from the window. Then she wished Jody were alive, and her father too. She took a few steps toward the dirty dishes in the sink but half-way there she slumped into a chair.

Twenty-four
I Learn About Bass

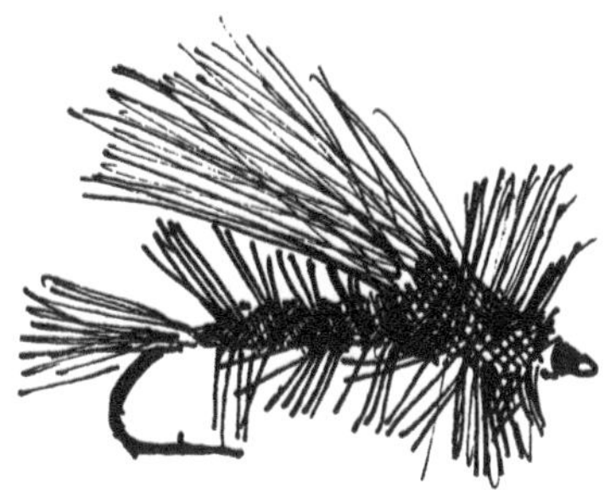

For my birthday, Mother, Teri, Al, and I went into Milton for burgers at T.J.'s Diner and the cook had made a small cake with candles on it. We sat in one of the booths with the green leather upholstery. The walls of the booths were black-and-white checkerboard tiles, and photographs were plastered everywhere. Over our booth was a picture of the guy who built the diner in the 1930s. He was leaning on an old car parked along a road with a Route 66 sign next to him.

There were old jukebox wall boxes in each booth into which you could drop a quarter and pick out a song to be played over a PA system. Neither the wall boxes nor the jukebox worked, but it was fun to spin the knob on top and see the names of the songs. It was my favorite place to go to eat. Al had arranged it. The whole meal was his treat—my birthday present from him.

When we got back home, there were three presents for me to open. When I opened Al's gift—his second—I did not know what I was looking at. It was like a tiny portable writing desk.

"It's a fly-tying setup," Al said. "This here is the vice. See, in here are compartments for different kinds of feathers, thread, yarn, and here's a bottle of glue."

My eyes widened. "Wow."

"Al, that's too much," Mother said.

Al patted me on the shoulder. "You have worked so hard on your reading this summer, you deserve it. I will teach you how to tie flies this winter. Besides, it is sort of paying you back for reading *The Call of the Wild* to me."

"Thank you, Al," I said and gave him a quick hug. It was awkward because we had never touched except for a pat on the back or shoulder. I instantly wished I hadn't done it.

"Oh…" Al said with a laugh.

I changed the subject. "What is the next book you want me to read to you?"

"Do you mind staying with another dog related book for the next one?

"No, I don't mind. I liked the story about Buck, at least the parts I understood I liked."

"Okay then," Al said. "*Old Yeller* it is."

During August, Alton and I fished for bass in the lower stretches of the creek with big, gaudy flies. In the early afternoons, when the caddis and mayflies hatched together, Al taught me how to entice the bass to take flies on the water's surface. He would have me tie on an orange or brown Stimulator—a fly that mimics a lot of different insects. We would walk downstream to the wider, slower, deadwater where the bass live all year. Though Al was definitely a trout and salmon fisherman, he told me that pound-for-pound, smallmouth bass fight as hard as any fish.

Once the fly was tied to the tippet of my leader, I flipped a little roll cast under the bank on the opposite side of the creek. There was not much current there, so one mend of the line upstream and I had a pretty good drift of the fly, natural as could be.

Al leaned forward and tried to follow the drifting fly on the surface. "Just let it drift for a few feet," he said. When nothing took the fly, he said, "Now strip the line just a little. Make the fly move almost imperceptibly."

Just a little twitch, I thought. *That must be what he means.*

I did as he said, and before I was ready, there was an explosion at my fly—a bigger splash than I had anticipated. I stripped the line and set the hook solidly. The bass quickly ran, zig-zagged, and then jumped clear out of the water. We both got a good look at him.

"Yeah!" Al cried. "You got him."

I didn't get the fish on the reel where the drag could help me play him; I had the line between my right index finger and the rod's cork grip. I tried not to pinch the line too much so when the fish ran I could let some line slip through. This was the biggest fish I'd ever hooked. I knew if I did not give him some line when necessary, he would break off and be gone.

"Just a little pressure now," Al said, "move him side to side with the rod to disorient him."

I did just as he said, and the big bass jumped three more times. After, when I tried to pull him left, and then right again, I could see the fish lying on his side in the water.

"That's good," Al said. "Bring him in. We don't want to tire him out so much that we kill him."

I steered him close to the bank and Al knelt and grabbed the fishes lower lip with his thumb and forefinger and lifted him onto the bank. The orange Stimulator was stuck solidly in the corner of the fish's big mouth. Al quickly removed the fly, and, with his grip still on the bass's lip he held it up for me to inspect.

"Fourteen inches, at least," he said. "About a pound and a half. Here, you take him, just like I have his lip. Let's get him back in the water."

I stuck my thumb in the fish's mouth, and Al did not let go until he was sure I had him.

"Now lie on your belly if you have to and place him back into the water. But hold onto him to be sure he's not belly-up. Your whole hand will have to be in the water.

Again, I did as he said.

"Now, move him forward and backward to run some water through his mouth and gills. When he revives a bit, you'll feel him start to swim. Then you let go."

It was just like Al said. After a few seconds, the fish felt stronger in my hands, and when I let him go he swam slowly toward the far bank.

Alton said, "Great job! Wasn't that fun?" He gave me a high five, and I had to jump to reach his hand. "Sam, there are LOTS of bass in this creek, and they're a blast to catch on a fly rod."

I could hardly stand still.

"Now, this is important; 'lipping' bass like that with your thumb is a normal way to land and handle them. Their mouths are indestructible. But *never* do that to a trout or salmon … got that?"

"Why?" I asked.

"A trout or salmon's jaw is very fragile, and people who lip trout and then release them don't even realize that they've probably damaged the fish severely, and it will likely die in a day or so."

"We don't want that," I said.

Al looked at me and smiled. "You got that right."

Suddenly Al said, "Look at that! Do you see it?" He pointed downstream.

I peered into the water looking for a big fish, or the otter whose tracks we'd been seeing all summer. Then I did see it—a dead eel floating next to the bank. "Wow, that's much bigger than the eels we saw."

"That's no eel."

I looked up at Al, then back at the creature. It was thicker than the eels, and I could see it had a hideous head. Or should I say mouth…its mouth *was* its head, and its mouth was terrifying. "What *is* it?"

"That's a lamprey, or a sea lamprey. That's what my father called them."

Al picked up a stick and flipped the thing onto the bank. "Look at this mouth," he said.

I had never seen anything like it. Its mouth looked like a big suction cup with spiraling rows of dozens of sharp teeth. It looked as though if attached to something, it wouldn't let go.

"These are amazing fish," said Al. "See that hideous mouth?"

"I can't *not* see it."

"These fish are predatory—when they're not spawning. That mouth is like a suction cup that attaches them to other fish, and the teeth then engages the flesh of the poor host. Then they use their knife-like tongue to tear into the flesh and they suck blood and other fluids. Eventually, the lamprey is either knocked off by the host fish, or it lets go."

"Does the fish it attacks die?"

"They sometimes do, but some survive. Fish that survive a sea lamprey attack expend more energy on healing than on producing eggs and mating, which causes declines in fish populations."

"Then why do you say they're amazing?"

"Well, because they've been around pretty much unchanged for 350 million years. They've survived five mass-extinctions. I think that's amazing."

"Hmmm … I still think it's gross."

"Yes," Al laughed. "They do have a bad reputation, that's for sure. But know what else is interesting? They were once highly coveted as food, and probably still are in some parts of the world. I've even heard of the term 'jugged lampreys,' but I don't know what the 'jugging' consists of. I read once that lamprey meat is not easily digested by humans and that King Henry I of England died because he ate too many lampreys. Apparently, it was his favorite dish."

I squirmed a little and shook my head.

"No, me neither," Al responded. "I too have no interest in trying them. Though, I do enjoy crab, oysters, and clams—maybe I would like lamprey meat. Then again, I'd hate to end up like 'ole King Henry.

"This lamprey died a couple of weeks ago after spawning, which they all do. I'm surprised it's still here. Other fish feed on their carcasses."

Al looked around and up and down the river. "I guess the scavengers have heard Henry's story too."

Al held up the Stimulator by its eyelet and blew on it to dry it out, as I had seen him do many times. Then handed it to me. "Let's catch more bass!"

The rest of August we walked to the creek and fished for bass. It wasn't just me fishing now with Al offering fly fishing lessons. As the summer went on, we were fishing together, thirty or forty feet apart. Many times we would each have a fish on at the same time. Alton's eyes were getting worse, and he would sometimes ask me to tie on his smaller flies for him. He said it did not embarrass him, but I don't think he liked the idea. In the evenings, and after supper when the farm chores were done, I read to Alton on the porch. He never seemed to mind how poorly I did.

On the thirty-first of August, we walked to the clearing next to the creek to inspect the piles of peeled logs. They were a pretty golden color now and the many cracks and splits on the log ends suggested they had dried out a lot. Alton went to each pile and lifted up the ends of several logs and dropped them with a loud, wooden 'clunk.'

"It has been a nice, hot summer," he said. "I think they're dry enough." He stood with both hands on his hips and looked at each pile, and at the stakes in the middle where he said the cabin would go. "I'll talk to your mom about the cabin build … make sure it doesn't interfere with the farm work this fall."

We were actually going to do this. Build a log cabin at the creek!

Twenty-five
BUILD IT TO LAST

I did not read to Alton in September; we were too busy with the farm. But he did give me a stack of fishing articles to read on my own after chores and a very old book about log cabin construction, which had many illustrations.

When the pumpkins were all harvested and delivered to the hardware and grocery stores, and the plastic mulch was removed from the fields and the greenhouses were empty and cleaned out, we started the cabin. For a month, I had dreamed about building the cabin.

I had returned to school, so most of the construction would be done on the weekends, but Al said he would "putter around" the site, cleaning, sharpening tools, and doing small jobs.

"We want to get the walls up and the roof on before the snows come," Al said.

"What do you want me to do?"

Al nudged me with his shoulder. "You can build the thing, and I'll teach you how."

The first Saturday of the build we started slowly. We used the old tractor and Al's trailer to haul supplies and tools to the site.

Before we started anything, we sat on two of the cedar stumps that we had hauled to the site last spring. I counted them again. There were twelve, each one about two feet in diameter, but short, maybe sixteen inches in length.

"Log cabins are products of the forest," Al said. "If we do this right, it should appear to have grown out of the moss, trees, and fern. We have already picked the spot where we want to put it, inside of the four piles of logs, but there are other considerations to think about. Can you guess what they might be?"

I perked up. Even though my teachers said my reading had improved, they also had told me for years that I was "basically very smart," but I never felt smart. But *this* time I knew some of the answers. Or at least I thought I did. When I was re-reading about shelter-building in that old Boy Scouts manual, I memorized what was in the chapter about building site selection.

"Water drainage," I said, "water accessibility, and how should it be placed for the best view and sunlight, stable ground, and safety. And no tall, dying, or leaning trees over the site."

Al leaned back, looking at me.

"I read it in my manual." I stood tall. Without having to think it over, I snapped a correct answer to his question, and it felt great. *That's what Al has been talking about all summer,* I thought. *The power of reading.*

"Very good," Al said. He showed me his notebook. "I have made some notes and sketches for the cabin. Would you mind reading them for me? I brought the wrong glasses."

I hadn't read aloud to Al for over a month because of harvest time.

"Should con—con—consid-er..."

"Good, sound out the consonants," Al offered.

"...consider for the site the fall...following fac-tors: Water ass—ack—*ac-cess—a—ability,* drainage, safety, and sunlight."

I snapped a look up at Al. "That's exactly what I answered!"

Al nodded. "Good job. These cedar stumps we're sitting on, these will be the foundation of the cabin, and they are very important, just as reading is the foundation of knowledge."

That correct answer I had given a moment earlier showed me the way. I wanted to answer more things just like that in the future.

We then set to work measuring, both with long strings tacked to the stumps that have little "line levels" attached to them, and with very long measuring tapes.

He had me stand where I thought the cabin should sit and facing out of the imaginary door and front porch.

"You sure?" he asked.

"Yes."

"Okay. Looks good to me." He adjusted one of the stakes, sticking it in the ground between my feet. Then, we measured diagonals again and again until Al was satisfied.

In the trailer were many big, flat rocks. "I collected these from the ancient stone wall weeks ago. We'll set the cedar stumps on these. Don't worry, I checked with your Mom first."

"I wasn't worried."

We carried the stones over to where the cabin corners would be, and then in the middle distance of each future wall. Using shovels, we dug out level spots a few inches deep for the stones. Once they were all solid and level, we used the string levels on the corner stumps and made them level by marking two of them, which we had to shorten with the chainsaw. It was fun; in no time, we had eight stumps, which Al called *piers*, in place, and we could now see the footprint of the cabin. And the strings showed all the stumps, now of varying height, were level and square. We were on our way.

"The middle piers we will do later when we put in the floor. Let's take a lunch break. Then we'll start with the sill and end logs."

"The bottom four logs?" I asked.

"You got it."

After lunch, Alton re-adjusted the cedar stumps one more time. Once he was satisfied, we used tools with hooks on them that he called peavy's to roll and move the logs around. Al said a lot of people call a peavy a "*cant hook*," but that a peavy has a hook on the end whereas the 'cant hook' doesn't. "A peavy's a lot better," he said under his breath while hoisting a log.

With the peavys, we rolled the best, straightest logs up onto the cedar piers — two on opposite sides first, then we secured them in place with the sharp, metal log dogs. Alton measured diagonally again and then marked the edges of the stumps on the bottom of the logs. We then rolled the logs one-hundred-and-eighty degrees and secured them in place with the log dogs again. Using the chainsaw, Alton cut kerfs about four inches deep into the marked spots of the logs. Then he knocked the kerfs out and smoothed out the notches with a chisel and mallet. Once he had carved a notch on either end, we rolled the log back, and it plunked onto the cedar stumps. The notches fit perfectly. We did that with both longer sill logs, then with the shorter end logs. The end logs were rolled into place, 'dogged' so they would not move while marking, and they too were marked and notched.

The half-circle notches were a little trickier, and Al used the chainsaw to cut them out. He cut straight down into the marked notch on both sides of the log, about an inch apart, then he knocked the kerfs out with a hammer and, using the chisel, made each notch round and smooth. "I made this chisel out of a leaf-spring from a junked-out old Ford truck," he said. Once all four notches were finished, we un-dogged the end logs and rolled them back, making another loud plunk sound as the notches fit together.

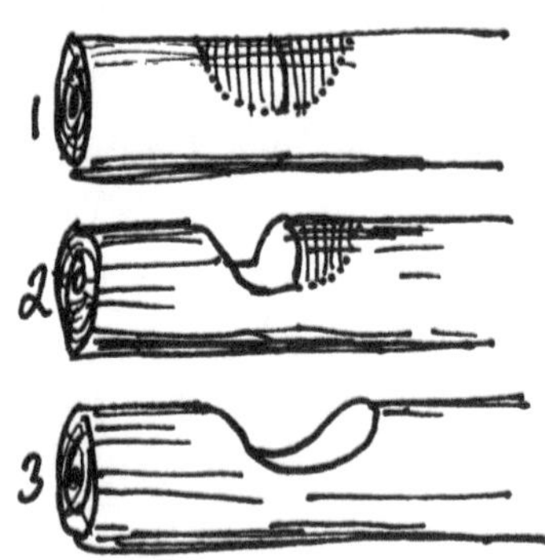

After measuring the diagonals yet again, Al dogged them in place. He took out an old hand drill with a large drill bit. "This is called a brace and bit," he said. He showed me how to use it and had me drill down into the top log about an inch and a half.

"We'll countersink all of these as we stack the logs," he said. "Then we will spike them."

After I drilled the countersink hole, Al drove a large 10-inch spike down into the log through to the cedar stump. Then he took a vice grip with a heavy bolt in the jaws, placed the threaded end of the big bolt on top of the spike, and, using a four-pound sledgehammer, drove the bolt and the spike further down into the countersink hole. The big flat head of the spike was down into the log over an inch.

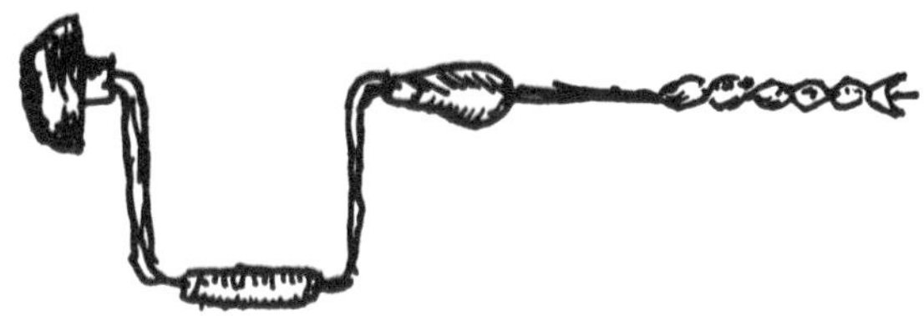

"Can you think of why we need to do this?" Al asked.

I shook my head.

"It's because the logs can shrink over time, especially after there's a roof over them, and they remain dry for many years. If the spike has not been countersunk, and the log shrinks, the head of the spike will push up into the log above it and mess up the wall's joints."

That made perfect sense, even to someone my age. But then, I was learning a lot. Before spiking the end logs onto the longer sill logs, Al measured the diagonals for what seemed like the twentieth time.

"It might seem like overkill," Al offered, "but I built a shed once in which the sills were out-of-square. Getting the roof on was a nightmare and took a lot of fudging."

"I see," I said.

"It's two o'clock. Do you want to quit for the day, or put up a couple of wall logs?"

"It's up to you," I said. "I'm just helping move logs around and drilling and hammering. Are you tired?"

"Let's do two more," he said.

We had to take the time with each wall log to knock off any knots or bumps that might keep it from lying flush with the log below. To do that meant rolling the logs several times. First, we cut the notches, rolled the log in place, and walked the length of the wall looking under the top log to see if the fit was good. Any place we could see where the log was being held up because of a knot or too much of a bend, Al would mark with a piece of chalk. Then we would roll it over with the peavy, dog it in place *again*, and shave down the chalked spots either with the hatchet or a tool called an adz (a tool that resembled a garden hoe, but with a heavy, sharp blade), then we'd roll it over again plunking the notches together. If the logs still didn't lie together nicely, and light was visible between the logs, Al would inspect the notches. Sometimes, he could fine-tune them by delicately, carefully deepening them using the tip of the chainsaw. Eventually we would get the logs to fit together perfectly. Then, I would drill the three-quarter inch holes for the spikes.

But before spiking the notches, Al would do two things: he would place the six-foot level vertically on what would be the inside of the cabin so the walls would go up straight and true, and he would make a mental note of where the previous spike was in the log below. We had to drill each new hole a little off-center so the new twelve-inch long spike wouldn't hit the head of the spike below. I never would have thought of that. There were so many little things such as that to learn, Al encouraged me to write them down in the journal he had given me. He didn't *make* me, but rather suggested I do it, which to me was almost the same thing.

We were both getting tired, so we quit. Once we gathered up all the tools and placed them in the wagon and had cleaned the site, we stepped closer to the stream and looked back at our work. I could hardly believe it. It looked like something real. It took little imagination to envision all the walls up.

"Wow," I said. "All that in only one day."

"Yep," Al said. "And if you're not too sore tomorrow, and by you I mean *me*, we might be able to put up a couple more courses. Each course is four logs."

"That would be great!" I said.

"Once all that fidgeting with the layout of the piers and the sill and end logs is finished, log cabins go up fast—twelve inches at a time."

Alton was right. The next day we both were a little sore, but we did put up eight more logs. In addition to using the level for every new log, every second or third log he remeasured the diagonals. "Let's try to keep the thing square," he kept saying.

We did forget to stagger the drill hole on one notch and the bit hit square onto the head of the spike below, but this wasn't Al's first cabin. "Not a problem," he said, and fetched from his toolbox in the wagon a bottle of glue. While he did that, I drilled a new hole.

"We don't want to have a little hole in the joint that might be inviting to insects, especially termites." Al collected a bunch of sawdust and using a slab of bark as a plate, mixed it with the glue. "We'll just make a slurry and pack it in the empty hole."

While Al packed the paste with a stick, I wrote the remedy in my journal.

When he was finished, Al saw me thumbing through my journal. He was straddling the wall, which was now over three feet tall.

"Sam, I want to say something to you."

Oh, jeez, what have I done? I thought.

"I just want to say that I'm really proud of how far you've come this year."

I squinted up at him.

"You're reading has improved a great deal this summer. And I know it's a lot of work."

I nodded. "It's still hard every time I read, but I can get through an article or a book now and feel confident that I understood it."

"Well, I recommend you keep at it, every day. You're a good young man, and I don't know if I've ever met a smarter boy your age, or one with more potential."

I did not know what to say to any of that. "Mom and the teachers talked a month ago. It's dyslexia."

"I know. I knew about the dyslexia."

"The teacher said you teaching me the sounds for letters I didn't know has helped a lot."

"It has helped me too. More than you can know. You know, some kids develop a 'learned helplessness' response; when they get to a word they can't figure out, they hang on it for a long time waiting for a parent or teacher to read it for them. I noticed early on that you didn't routinely do that, at least in the time we've known each other. That also makes me proud of you. You don't give up. That's important because you have to manage it for all your life."

I looked at him. "There is no cure?"

"Sam—don't worry. No, there's no 'cure' in the sense you're thinking, but in no way should it hold you back. Not with good support and effort on your part. Remember, you just have to read every day and learn to *manage* it. And you have your Mom and Teri, the best support group you can have."

"And you," I said. "I have you."

"Yes, you have me."

A tear rolled down my cheek and I quickly wiped it away.

Alton jumped down and sat on the log next to me. He put his arm around my shoulder and said, "It's okay, Sam. You have all of us, and your teachers, now that they know what's going on, and you also have the most important thing: your desire to read and to learn. Those things are all you'll need. Trust me."

"It's cool," was all I could say. I tried to make out like I wasn't too upset. I stared at the ground and then looked up at the creek. "And fishing. I have fly fishing, thanks to you."

"Let's clean up and head home."

As we picked up the tools, chalk, and our lunch pails, Al kept talking. "Who invented the light bulb, Sam?"

I knew this answer well. "Thomas Alva Edison."

"Dyslexic."

"Really?"

"Yup. Who invented the telephone?"

We had learned about those guys in school. "Alexander Graham Bell."

"Dyslexic."

I couldn't believe it was so.

"Have you heard of Leonardo da Vinci? Albert Einstein? Galileo?"

"Of course."

"Dyslexics, all of them."

"How about Picasso, Muhammed Ali, Walt Disney, and even President Woodrow Wilson."

I stood still, as if I was frozen in time. "Are you kidding me?"

"Nope. All dyslexics. The point is, Sam, you aren't afflicted, but you do have a glitch to overcome. And just like Einstein and Mr. Edison, it's not anything that will hold you back, not if you don't let it. And as far as I can see, you're not going to let it, and that's why I'm proud of you."

We glanced at the cabin site before getting on the tractor, just as we had the day before. The walls were nearly as high as my chest already.

"Four more workdays," Al said, "and I think the walls may be finished."

I looked back at the cabin site again. Alton had been right. It was going up fast.

I climbed onto the tractor, and Al sat on the back of the trailer. Before I started the engine, I said, "This winter, when I read to you, I'd like to try something other than a dog story. They were great, but I'm ready for something else."

Alton folded his arms over the lunchpail in his lap and braced himself for the trailer ride back to the farmhouse. "Steinbeck it is," he said with a smile. "And after him, Jim Harrison, and then, Annie Proulx."

Twenty-six

The Walls Go Up

I lay awake that Sunday night. Sore and tired, I cast my memory back as far as it would go, and I realized no man had ever said he was proud of me, at least that I could remember. I was glad Alton felt that way, but I also felt weighted with responsibility. I knew I was no Einstein, and I did not want to let him, Mom, or Teri down.

By the end of the following weekend, we had all four cabin walls up, six rafters were notched and set into the top logs, and the roof plate was in place. Al spent as much time measuring the plate—the flat boards on top of each wall that the roof would be attached to—as he had the sill and end logs. "The plates too have to be perfectly square and even on all sides, just like the foundation." The rafters, he said, would not only help stabilize the walls, but can be used to build a loft overhead for a sleeping area or for storage.

"The next weekend that we work, we'll stick a roof on 'er," Al said.

"But I was thinking," he continued, "since we've made such great progress in just two weeks, and the farm has been put to bed, maybe we ought to ask your mom if we can go salmon fishing for one day."

"I've never fished for salmon!"

"I know, but it's up to your mom. She invited me for supper tonight, so we can ask her together. But remember if she says 'no,' understand that she may have her own reasons."

"Okay."

We washed up and Al went to the kitchen. "Smells great, Rachel. What can I do to help?"

"Umm, if you can fill the water glasses, that'd be great."

We had my favorite meal: roast chicken, baked potatoes, and green beans from the garden. Teri breezed in from the porch.

"Howdy, howdy! How's everyone?"

Alton was closest, so she hugged him first, then Mother and me.

"I haven't seen you since your artist retreat," Al said. "How was it?"

"Oh, it was wonderful. We each had a little cabin a short walk from the water, and there was a huge studio to work in filled with any and all art supplies we could want, which was a nice change. I created a new piece that I think is my favorite."

"I can't wait to see it," Al said.

"Speaking of cabins," Teri said, "how is yours coming?"

"They go up fast, log cabins," I said, "twelve inches at a time." Al winked at me.

"I haven't seen the progress either," Mother said. "But I've heard a lot of chainsaw noise coming from the creek."

"No?" Teri asked. "Why not?"

"I've been manning the pumpkin stand every day. We've sold almost all the 'mums' already."

"Oh," Teri said. "That reminds me. We had a little contest on the last day of the retreat when we had one hour to start and finish a piece of art in our medium. When the time was up, we all voted, and the winner received a new easel. I couldn't find anything for a subject, so I painted from memory one of those blood-red chrysanthemums you've been growing in No. 2."

"I bet it was tough to do in pastels," Al said.

Teri winked at Al as she sipped from her coffee cup. "The easel is in my car."

"Congratulations!" Mother said. Teri sat back in her chair and smiled.

Al nodded at Teri, and she smiled at him.

Teri was different. She was above feeling pride, but she exuded an enviable confidence. She was always, as Mother liked to say, straightforward. I think Al liked that about her. As for me, I just loved her for everything she was. Besides Al, she and Mother were the only ones who encouraged me to keep reading, but yet always accepted me for better or worse. That is, they were the only ones until Alton Sands walked up Dibbin Creek and into our lives. Now I had three people.

"About the cabin," Al said. "Sam's right. They go up fast once the first course of logs are in place. We already have the walls up and the plates are on."

"Seriously?!" Mother said.

"Indeed. With one long weekend, I think we can have the roof on."

"That reminds me," Mother said. "I've seen you bring lumber on your trailer. I want to pay you for that. I don't want you spending money."

Al waved his hand. "No, no… over the decades, I've helped many people build different structures. When the projects were finished, they would often give me left-over building materials which I stored in my barn. I'm happy to finally get rid of some of it."

"If you're sure," Mother said.

"My pleasure." Al paused. "Anyway, since Sam and I have come so far so quickly, we thought at this point we'd like to get the roof on before you two see it. We've already cut out the door, and all that will be left will be to cut sections out where we want windows, which I also have in my barn, and to chink the walls between each of the logs. That's a nice late fall/early winter job. Maybe we could have a big reveal, and cook a lunch at the creek."

Mother and Teri looked at each other. "Sound's great," Mother said.

Teri slung her arm around me and squeezed me tight. She did that a lot, sometimes for no reason.

After supper was finished, Alton and I washed the dishes. Mother and Teri went to the living room and talked. I overheard Mother saying how much Al had helped me with my reading. I worried if he heard her talking, he might get embarrassed, so I kept asking Al silly questions like: *Had he ever grown crops before? How old was he when he started fly fishing? And how long had he had his old Jeep?*

He patiently answered all of the questions.

After the dishes, we entered the living room. Teri was sprawled out on one of the couches, and Mother was slumped in one of the overstuffed chairs and had her feet up on a magazine rack. We did not own a footstool. It looked strange; I didn't see her with her feet up very often.

"Mom," I asked, "would it be okay if I showed Alton Dad's office?"

"Of course. And Al, I should have thought of this before, but if you see any books you haven't read, you're welcome to borrow them."

"Many thanks."

"Follow me, Al." We walked up the stairs and opened the door of the office, a place where I would sit for many, many hours when I was younger. During the past summer, I had been so busy I had not often visited it.

Alton stood in the doorway of the office. The old man looked warmly at the floor-to-ceiling bookcases covering three walls. He walked up to the desk and looked at the guitars hanging behind it on the only wall free of bookcases. Surrounding the two guitars were watercolors from around the world, some were unfinished, and mountaineering photographs that were slightly yellowed with age. There were two shadowboxes: one filled with insects, the other with a small, taxidermied bat. Alton leaned in to inspect the contents of the single shelf attached to the wall directly above the desk. It held all manner of trinkets and tiny souvenirs, including some small stones with writing on them.

As he looked sideways at the spines of the hundreds of books, some of which were very old, I broke the quiet.

"I like to come up here and look at all the books. My dad must've been a good reader."

"Well, I admire his taste in books."

After a moment, I said, "This house is a hundred-and-fifty years old. Teri says it has friendly ghosts."

Alton smiled but kept reading book spines.

Then I said something that I realized was silly but once I started I couldn't stop. "Sometimes I come up here and just look around. I imagine there's a special book somewhere on the shelves and that if you pull it out, a secret door opens up into another world." I laughed quietly and awkwardly at the childishness of it.

But Alton didn't laugh. He turned to me, put his hand on my shoulder, and said, "Sam … *all* books do that."

Then, he reached and pulled a small book off the shelf. He inspected the spine and smiled. He handed it to me.

"I think you're ready for this, Sam. We'll put Steinbeck on hold."

"*Oliver Twist* by Charles Dickens." I said the title without hesitation. "I've tried Dickens before a couple of times at school. I couldn't do it."

"I figured. But you can now, my friend. No problem."

Al didn't ask me to try reading it now, but I thumbed open the pages, and read aloud the first paragraph. I struggled with 'fictitious,' and had to ask what 'to wit' meant, and stumbled again with 'inasmuch,' but the rest of the paragraph was fine. Then I said something that surprised both of us.

"Al, I read aloud to you all summer, would you mind reading a couple of paragraphs to me? Just this once?"

"More than fair," Al said, taking the book from me. He settled into my dad's old chair, and I sat on the window seat. Once he found his reading glasses, Al read deliberately, but with a beautiful rhythm and ease, as if they were his words.

"For a long time after it was ushered into this world of sorrow and trouble by the parish surgeon, it remained a matter of considerable doubt whether the child would survive to bear any name at all; in which case it is somewhat more than probable that these memoirs would never have appeared; or, if they had, that being comprised within a couple of pages, they would have possessed the inestimable merit of being the most concise and faithful specimen of biography, extant in the literature of any age or country."

As he read, I closed my eyes and leaned back on a cushion. I had to focus hard on every word, every syllable; distraction was always my enemy. But I did. I focused, and listened, and it was beautiful. *If I could only read like that,* I thought.

We returned to the living room and Al said, “Young Sam is going to tackle Dickens.”

“Very nice,” Mother responded.

“I have to go,” Al offered, “but before I do, I wanted to see how you felt about my taking Sam to the big river this Saturday for a little salmon fishing. I know the water well, and there are a couple of productive spots that are not dangerous to wade. I would be right next to him the entire time.”

Before Mother could answer, he added, “Of course, if you’re not comfortable with that, Sam and I agree that we will understand.”

Again before Rachel could answer, Teri interjected. “Al, is there a back seat in the Jeep?”

“There is indeed, a small one.”

“If you’d just be going for the day, and if there’s room, I’d love to go along to do some sketching.”

“That would be wonderful,” Al said.

Then, all three looked at Rachel. “Of course you can go—and you too.” (Smiling at Teri.) “And don’t worry about me; I’ll just stay here and mind the farm.”

Alton felt bad. “We could take another car so all four can go—”

“No, I’m kidding. I have a lot of shopping and puttering I’d like to do. It’ll make it easier if I don’t have to make lunches in the middle of the day.”

“Great,” Teri said. “You can make mine the night before. Remember I like sourdough for my sandwich.”

Mother laughed and flashed a hand gesture at Teri that I was not allowed to do.

Then Al turned to me. “Sam, remember, you can make it easier for your mom if you get your weekend homework done Friday night.”

“Yes, I’ll try.”

Al’s Jeep rattled out the driveway and down the road. I went back up to my dad’s office, sat in his chair, and started *Oliver Twist* from the beginning. It was hard, but I knew I had to stick to it. And I knew it would be worth it.

Twenty-seven
SALMON FLIES & MEMORIES

The old Jeep wasn't the most comfortable ride, and we had to stop three times to stretch our legs. I rode in the back seat and my butt kept falling asleep. After driving for two hours, the farm country gave way to the heavily forested lands of logging country. The trees were much bigger and the forests thicker than around home. We drove past several streams that looked very fishy, and all were bigger than Dibbin Creek. Eventually, we met the river and drove alongside it, traveling upriver for about half a mile. Then Alton pulled into a gravel area close to the riverbank.

This was no farm creek; it was more like a lot of water barreling down a gorge. Large boulders the size of dump trucks were everywhere, and the river smashed and splashed into them causing rapids on each side of the rock, only to crash into another boulder a few yards farther downriver. I didn't say a word, but stared at the river and wondered how could I ever wade into that. It looked like it would sweep me away, and it all looked over my head.

"It's beautiful," Teri said. "I came here once before, Sam, with your dad, before he met your mom."

Teri wasn't afraid of the river. She wasn't afraid of anything. Then again, she wasn't fishing. She grabbed her art supplies and her new easel from the Jeep.

"We'll rig up our rods when we get to our spot," Al said, "but we have to walk up this trail for a bit to where we'll fish."

Teri followed the path with us. We walked for about fifteen minutes, skirting the river. Finally, we stopped. Here the river, still rolling along, wasn't quite as—what's the word—*violent* as where we parked. And here, I could see the bottom for about twenty feet from the bank.

"This is called The Warden Pool," Al said. Then he exclaimed, "Oh! Look there, about forty feet out."

I gulped and rubbed my eyes and looked again and began to shake all over. Salmon were rising all alongside a foamy seam in the river. They looked like dolphins swimming alongside a ship. Rolling up, breaking the water, and gracefully diving again. There were many of them rising, sometimes several at once. They were bigger than anything I'd caught and were silvery and they looked like they would eat my fly if I could get it out to them.

"See how they're rising like porpoises?" Al asked. "Emergers. They're taking caddis emergers just as the flies get to the surface when they're most vulnerable. Rig up your rod, and I'll get a fly out for you."

My hands trembled as I jointed my rod. I tried to string the loop of fly line but kept missing guides because I couldn't stop trying to watch the fish rising.

"Take your time," Al said in a soft voice. "They'll still be there."

Twice I had to start all over again, but I finally rigged the rod and somehow got a little emerger fly tied on.

We waded in up to my belt, just slightly upriver from one of the rising fish. The water was very cold, and I winced when it hit my gonads. Al snickered, "Yes, it'll wake you up."

Al whispered to me. "Pay out a little line, and flip a roll cast about ten feet above where he's rising—you see the spot?"

I nodded and did as he said. The line shot out through the guides, and the fly landed almost directly above the fish. I thought the roll cast was too short by a couple of feet, but a fish smashed the fly, ate it, and shot upriver. I raised the rod tip slightly. He took line off my reel, and I suddenly realized I did not know what to do.

"We have to wade upstream with him," Al said. He was no longer whispering.

The rocks were slippery under my old sneakers that I had brought for wading, but Al kept reassuring me and with his hand gripping the back of my belt, he guided me in a little shallower. "We can fight him from here," he said quite loudly. When I lifted the rod high, with the handle over my head, Al placed his hand on my arm and lowered my rod.

He calmly said, "You only need to raise the reel above your head when a fish runs straight toward you. If you do it at any other times, you're doing it wrong. Don't worry, you're doing great!"

For the first few minutes, the fish did not leap once, but once he did jump, he seemed to be out of the water more than he was in it. I lost count of the jumps. Al had told me on the drive up that when a salmon leaps, I should lower my rod tip lust a little. He said I needed to "bow to the salmon." Every time he landed from a leap, he tried to shoot upstream some more. I heard Teri yell, "Yeah!" from the trees.

We kept wading upstream with him and finally the fish stopped under an overhanging bank and would not budge. I took a breath and Al said, "Give him about ten seconds, and then, lower the rod tip. Shove the butt of the rod into your belly and pull the rod sideways to the right—upstream. We'll try to move him off that spot before he gets a rest." I was shaking.

I didn't have to pull hard and the salmon was off and running again, not very fast, but more like a deliberate swim. Al knew what he was doing. When I pulled to the right, he took off to the left which put him directly opposite us in the river.

The fish made a couple of more leaps and a short run and suddenly gave up and quit altogether. When he did, Al said "Reel! Steady—not too fast. Just be ready to get your hand off the reel if he takes off again." I reeled in line, but he didn't run again. He was too tired. He came wallowing over to where we stood in about a foot-and-a-half of quiet water, and Al slipped his net under him and stood up slightly, breathing hard and grinning like a little kid. He kept the fish in the net but made sure he was in the water. I stepped toward them. Teri was whistling on shore holding her camera.

Al told me how to hold his tail with one hand and cradle his belly with my other.

"He's six pounds if he's an ounce," Al said, still grinning. "Keep him in the water; wait until Teri says she's ready. Ready, Teri?" he yelled.

"Ready!"

"Okay. Look up at Teri and lift him out of the water."

When I did, I was shocked. I wasn't prepared for how heavy the fish was once it was out of the water. I held its tail with one hand and supported its belly with my other. I tried not to squeeze him, but though he was tired he was still fighting — squirming and bending his body sideways trying to get free from my grip. I had held dogs and cats that were trying to get away, but nothing prepared me for how strong this wild salmon was. I could feel his strength and determination in my fingers. His big mouth was gasping for air.

"Alright," Al said. "I'll show you how to resuscitate him."

"We're not keeping him?"

"Not your first salmon. Of course it's your choice, but I think you should let him go, give back to the river."

I nodded. "Karma."

"I'll show you." Al took the salmon from me and, cradling him as I did, he placed him underwater and pointed his nose into the river's current. He moved the fish forward and back over and over, like we had done with my first bass. "He's a beaut. You did wonderfully, Sam. See his gills moving? I'm moving water through them. As soon as I feel him in my hands trying to swim, I'll let go with my cradle hand."

Alton tried it a few times, but each time the big fish rolled over on its side. Finally, it stayed upright. Holding just its tail, Al kept moving it in the water. Then, as if nothing had happened, it swam slowly off and out of sight.

"Now he'll sulk behind a rock on the bottom for a while and rest," Al said.

Then Al turned to me and shook my hand. I turned toward the bank and looked at Teri. Still holding her camera in one hand, she gave me a thumb's up and flashed her big, beautiful smile. I noticed my heart wasn't pounding now. At that moment, I felt like I had come very far. In that moment I felt the weight of all the things I had learned over the summer. I felt…different.

I took a splashing step forward and hugged Al with one arm. "That was amazing!"

"Yes, that was a fine fish," Al said.

"Sorry … I'm probably too old to hug people. Got caught up in the moment."

Teri yelled out, "Sam, don't worry about it! We're never too old!"

Over the next hour, we caught only two more small salmon that were about sixteen inches long and then broke for lunch. Teri had found a perch up on some tall rocks and made some sketches and she climbed down to join us. After lunch, the caddis that had been emerging had cooled off, so we hiked upriver to where a small creek flowed into the river and caught a dozen or so brook trout. By midafternoon, it was getting hot and we started back for the farm. We sang along with oldie songs on the radio all the way back except for when we stopped in the town of Centerville for ice cream cones.

I knew before we got home it was a day I'd never forget.

Twenty-eight
NEW ANIMALS & PERFORMANCES

It took Alton and me two weekends to get the roof on, slower than we had anticipated. Partly because I had a lot of homework to do, which of course was the priority, and partly because once we started I think Al realized he wasn't as fast working on a ladder as he once was. But he moved along just fine when we put in the floor; we finished the entire job in only four hours.

It was a small roof. Even so, the shingling took us an entire Sunday. But, once finished, the cabin was a beautiful thing. Golden yellow logs shone starkly against the dark forest behind, and it looked warm and inviting.

We told Mother and Teri we would have the big reveal on a Sunday in two weeks, weather permitting. That would give us time to do some finish work and build a door, and Alton had brought a dolly and an old, small woodstove and some stovepipe that he said was sitting in his barn when he bought his place almost fifty years ago. He also found a huge piece of slate somewhere for the stove to rest on.

It wasn't easy, but we somehow got everything finished. On the day of the reveal, Al had swung himself up onto the old tractor and drove it with the trailer to the farm porch. Mother, Teri, and I mounted the trailer. Teri called out, "Let's kick this pig," and the tractor lurched and bounced toward the creek. We didn't call it *the site* any longer, now it was referred to as the cabin. We had made so many trips with the tractor since last spring that there was now a dirt road that followed around the edge of the bottom field and through the ancient rock wall. Long ago, Al and I had removed the stones from the wall and rearranged them, and even made a makeshift gate out of some small, peeled logs. As we turned the corner into the clearing, Mother put her hand over her mouth.

"Good Lord," Teri gasped.

We all hopped off the trailer and Mother took a couple of steps and stopped, stunned by the moment. Teri walked closer to the cabin with her hands on her hips, then she turned and looked at the creek sliding along through the cedars and fir trees.

Mother stood next to Alton and started crying. She put her arm around his waist, and he put his around her shoulders. He whispered, "What's wrong, Rachel?"

"Before Jody died, we said we were going to build a cabin on the creek, for a little retreat from the farm."

"Oh, yes, Sam mentioned that. Well, here it is."

Mother sniffed and collected herself. "It's beautiful. You two did a wonderful job."

"We still have to build the porch," Al said, "and the porch roof. Yesterday, I stopped by and hooked up the woodstove. It's working great."

"Woodstove? Wow."

"Let's check out the inside," Al said, picking up a piece of carpenter's chalk.

All four of us went through the doorway. The fir flooring looked great, and the woodstove was in the far corner. Next to it was an old wooden box with about a dozen sticks of split firewood in it. I went over and looked at it.

"That box was in my barn also."

I looked up at Al. "You were busy yesterday."

"It was fun. I found some old, recycled barn boards. I had to run a metal detector over them to check for old nails, then I ran them all through my planer to make them all the same thickness. They make a nice loft, I think."

We all looked up. There was an old aluminum ladder leaning against the wall to get up to a loft Al had built one day while I was at school.

"I thought we could make a rustic wooden ladder next weekend," Al said, "and get the windows cut out and installed. All that would be left is to chink between the logs and build whatever you folks want for a porch. We can do that anytime.

"Speaking of windows, while we're all together, I hoped we could mark out where you would like them."

"Sure," Mother said. "Teri, you're the creative one and Sam and Alton, you built it, I think you three should decide by committee."

"No," I said. "Mom, you should decide. We built it for you.

All she could do is nod her head as she ran her fingers over some of the peeled logs.

We all sat on stumps and ate sandwiches. The conversations had slowed when suddenly Alton said, "Shhh! Stay still! Without anyone getting up, look upstream."

Frozen in place, each of us turned our heads up the creek. What looked like two beavers were swimming downstream toward the big pool in front of the cabin.

"Beavers?" I whispered.

"No, not beavers. It's the otters I've waited all summer to see. Remember the mud slides I showed you along the creek banks, Sam? And the tracks we saw?"

"Oh, yes."

Mother and Teri, smiling, watched in silence and stillness.

Finally Mother whispered to Al, "All the years I've lived here, I've never seen a river otter."

"They have a big range. I bet their main home is a couple of miles up the creek at Hermon Pond."

The otters made it into the pool as we remained still. They both dove under water.

Al said softly. "They know we're here, but if we sit still they won't get too alarmed."

When the animals surfaced, they frolicked around in the pool, touching each other, swimming apart, and rejoining. They hugged, rolled in the water, then dove separately again. After a few minutes of playing, though they might've been looking for fish when they were underwater, they both surfaced near the bank on the opposite side of the pool and pulled their sleek bodies out of the water. One of them sat scratching its side with its hind foot like a cat, while the other slid its belly along a fallen log before both disappeared into a dark hole at the base of a cedar tree where the bank had eroded and the roots were exposed.

"That was so cool," Teri said.

Alton stood up and walked to the creek and stared at the hole under the root system. "Good Lord, I never noticed it. All this time."

"Al?" Mother asked.

He looked at her and smiled. "It's a holt."

"A … *holt*?"

"Yes. That's what an otter den is called. I'll be darned. I imagine all the chainsaw work scared them off for a while." Then Al returned to his stump. "Otters don't like much human disturbance. They must like that spot a lot to return to it, being so close to the cabin. Of course, they have other holts around their territory. Think of that—a log cabin sharing a creek pool with an otter holt. Amazing."

We talked about otters for a while, and then circled the cabin several times and marked out the future windows. We decided to build the porch in the one obvious place, facing the creek.

The next two months saw the finished construction of the cabin. When it came time to chink the walls to make the building weather-tight, all four of us did it together. Al made four rough-cut tamps out of some maple wood he had and scrounged up some old wooden mallets. The tamps looked like big spatulas, except entirely made of wood. On each, the end opposite the handle was five or six inches long and tapered down to three-eighths inch thick. Al showed us how to use them to pound in the oakum. The oakum, long strips of woven hemp that was soaked in creosote, was the hardest thing to find. But, of course, Alton found some somewhere.

Before we started pounding the oakum between the logs, Al had harvested about forty-five ten foot long alders from up the creek. Once stripped of bark, Al used the hatchet and a tool called a 'froe' to split them into quarters lengthwise. Then we had a huge pile of 'quarter rounds,' which we nailed into the logs to reinforce the oakum. The quarter rounds didn't need to dry out like the big logs.

"If we don't nail the quarter rounds in between the logs inside and out," Al told us, "mice and squirrels will pull the oakum out for nest material, or the shrinking and expanding of the logs over time will make it fall out."

Once everything was finished, we all collected old chairs and things from our barns and purchased things from yard sales. The cabin soon had a fold-out sofa bed, and a little table big enough for four people to eat at or play cards. There were a few kerosene lamps, and even a tiny sink for which Al and I dug a small but elaborate leach pit. There were two Adirondack and two rocking chairs on the porch, and Mother and I wrestled a futon mattress up into the loft and we added a tiny end table. Downstairs, the wall that was the back of the cabin had only one small window, and it had the sofa bed along it. The rest of that wall was almost entirely covered with bookshelves and storage shelves. Then Al and I dug a hole and built an outhouse.

It was a beautiful cabin, and we all four loved it. But we could not think of a suitable name. We tried 'Otter Slide,' 'Dibbin Cabin,' 'The Reading Room …' but nothing we came up with worked. We all figured a name would come to us at some point.

Thanksgiving came and went. Al had offered to cook the turkey and showed up at six o'clock in the morning to start it.

I worked hard on my reading all fall and winter, spending hours each day reading and practicing working through and sounding out the syllables of every difficult word. Some days were harder than others, but clearly, I had improved. It simply took practice and determination and a lot of help from Alton. I continued to write and draw in my journal, though, to be honest, my spelling wasn't much better than my reading, but that too improved with practice.

I also tried to improve at tying flies. I had four that I could tie as well as any I saw in stores: Wooly Buggers, Elk Hair Caddis, Adams, and Stimulators. Mom was kind enough to buy some fly-tying hooks and materials for me. I knew we seldom had any money left over after paying monthly bills, but she said I helped so much on the farm the last few years that she owed me. Which, of course, she didn't.

At Christmas, all four of us were together again. Our Christmas's weren't like many other people's. We only exchanged one or two gifts, but we put on short skits, sang carols (Mom played the dulcimer very well), watched *It's a Wonderful Life* every year, cooked a fancy meal, told stories, and Mom and Teri read poems or favorite passages from novels.

And this was a truly great Christmas. The past November, Al had picked me up a few times and drove me to his workshop and he helped me build for Mother what he called an Ottoman (I only knew it as a footstool) so she would have something to put her feet up on. He also had a huge slab of rock maple, so I made Teri a wide cutting board in the shape of a pig for her kitchen. (She was at our house every day, so I wasn't sure if she *had* a kitchen.) Al helped me wood burn my name and the date on one side.

For Al, I had asked Mother to buy a ten-dollar fly box from a store in Milton, and I filled it with several of each of the four flies I could tie. For wrapping paper I had cut up a brown paper bag and Teri painted on it a tree and a flying bird. It was her idea. She said it would mean more to Al than if I used store-bought Christmas paper. He carefully opened the gift and examined the flies. He seemed quite touched and gave me a high-five, then he folded the wrapping and put it in his pocket.

It was very clear that he was glad to be a part of this 'weird family,' as Teri called us. And it probably was a little weird, but it was *my* family. I could not imagine any holiday or important event without both Alton and Teri.

Yes, that Christmas *was* wonderful; everyone loved their gifts, Mother played the dulcimer so beautifully it brought tears to Al's eyes, and Teri, who perhaps had too much alcohol with her eggnog, put on a one-person play about '*The Wooden Shoes of Little Wolff*' and became so wrapped up in the performance she got a little too enthusiastic and tripped and broke a lamp. Once he knew Teri wasn't hurt, it was the first time I heard Alton laugh uncontrollably. When Mother told Al he too had to recite something or tell a story, he explained to me that Teri's play was based on a French tale, and he said the title in French: *Les Sabots de Petit Wolff.* Then he told the story of the origin of the word 'Sabotage,' that disgruntled factory workers wearing sabots—wooden shoes—came into play throughout European history, disrupting factory production in various ways. Not very Christmasy, but interesting.

Lying in bed that night, I felt I was a very different person than I was only twelve months earlier.

Twenty-nine
A Rest Under a Cedar

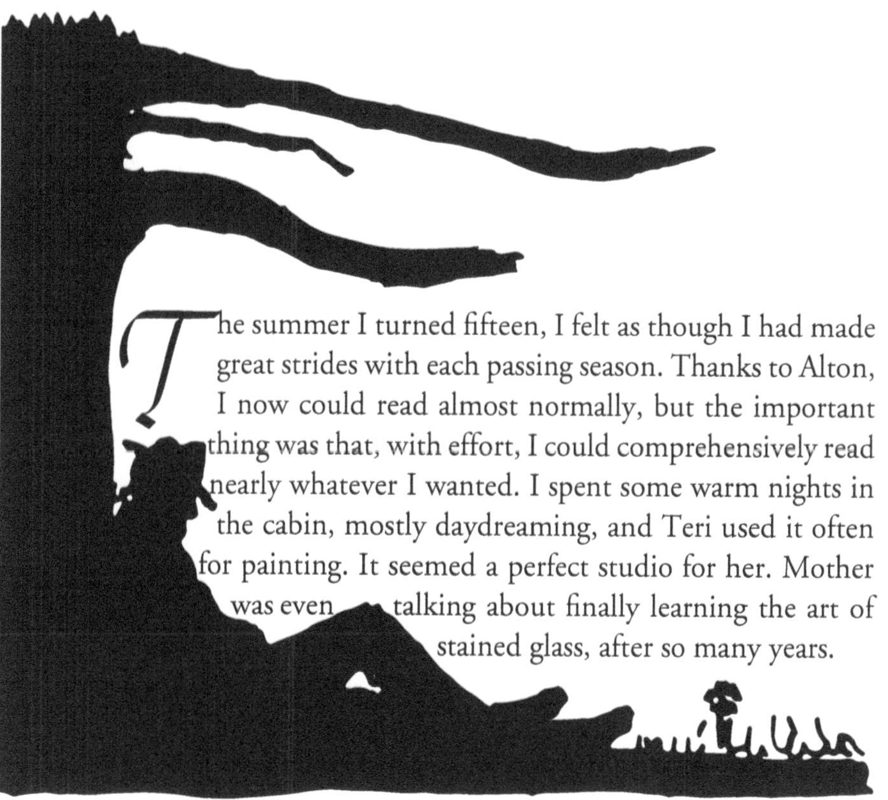

The summer I turned fifteen, I felt as though I had made great strides with each passing season. Thanks to Alton, I now could read almost normally, but the important thing was that, with effort, I could comprehensively read nearly whatever I wanted. I spent some warm nights in the cabin, mostly daydreaming, and Teri used it often for painting. It seemed a perfect studio for her. Mother was even talking about finally learning the art of stained glass, after so many years.

It had become pretty obvious to me that I was a year or two behind my mates at school because I had not been able to read at an early age. But now my grades in all subjects were very good. I had another nice birthday party in July, this time at the cabin. We had a picnic and later drove again to Milton for ice cream. Alton brought up the subject of college, and Mom and Teri put their two cents in.

A biologist? Teacher? A fishing guide? (I thought of the guiding one but dared not mention it.) Mom had high hopes for me and said she knew I could be whatever I wanted to be, but she also knew she had no college fund. I would have to work to earn tuition money.

Before Teri and Al left for their homes, Alton and I made plans to try for salmon in the big river in five days. "I'll be around before then," he said. "I'll probably fish the creek in a couple of days for bass to loosen my arm up a little. It's been aching the past few days, and I want to be able to strip line well if I hook a salmon."

We all hugged goodbye.

Three days went by, and I didn't see Al down at the creek. I called him to finalize plans for the salmon trip but only got his message machine.

But Alton *was* on the creek casting bushy flies for bass. He had worked his way up from the road to about a hundred yards downstream from the cabin where he knew some big bass lived under the opposite cut bank. He made a complicated sidearm cast and deftly skipped the Muddler Minnow fly under the overhanging bushes on the far bank. Before the Muddler could sink, a large bass hit it with a huge splash. Al stripped line and set the hook solidly. The fight was on, but as he stripped line to hold the fish, Al's arm hurt more than ever.

Al held the rod tightly. He looked down at his left hand. The bass was pulling hard and jumped twice, but now Al wasn't playing the fish. He knew something wasn't right. He suddenly felt awful. His fingers weren't working properly. They were cramping and the fly line was running out unrestricted. Al looked around. Twice he glanced at the ground behind him. Five feet away was an old cedar tree. For the next few seconds, he went through the motions of playing the fish, which he had done thousands of times before. He became very lightheaded and felt like his legs were going out from under him. The fly line fell from his left hand as the arm cramped against his torso. "Oh…!" he exclaimed. A terrible pain in his chest was followed by an enormous pressure. He dropped the rod and staggered backward. He tried to walk. He tried to take a step toward the cabin and the path to the farm, but he couldn't.

Alton dropped the rod and reached out with his right arm and touched the cedar tree. The pain was getting unbearable and now it was in his neck and jaw and his face contorted and strained. He had never felt this anxious—even when Alice died. He somehow spun himself around and, pressing his back against the tree, slid down it, sitting on the mossy ground. He leaned back against its trunk, trying to catch his breath, his chest heaving in-and-out. He sat, his right arm holding his left by the elbow, and looked up. He was drenched in sweat. He realized what was happening. He felt as though he had had the wind knocked out of him and his mouth opened and closed like a fish out of water.

Suddenly, a relief from the pain wash over him. Al stopped trying to catch his breath. He looked up through the branches of the tree and saw the sunlight streaking through them. It was warm—warmer than usual.

Al's mind oddly turned to other thoughts. At first, all he could see was Alice's face. But he was not worried about her. He worried about Sam, and Rachel, and Teri but at the same second he knew they would be okay. A vision of his parent's faces flashed before him, and nothing but love and wonderful memories flooded his mind. He could see the cedar tree, and the creek, and his home, and the cabin and the farm, and himself, napping in the warm sunlight filtered through the branches. He felt *good*, as though he was younger and new again. He could see everything in his life, bathed in a light that made everything look sharper. All of the loss, pain, and discomfort he had felt in nearly eight decades were swept away in an instant. He was at peace.

Al looked up through the branches again. The streaking sunlight was more abundant than before and getting brighter; more lovely. He saw the branches of the tree fold back, curling inward one by one until they were no more—there was only light. He suddenly felt more loved than he ever had and the light gave him clarity. The light made him understand that he would soon know what his reason for living was. He was overwhelmed by the beauty of it all, and his worries about his farm family were gone. The light made him understand they too would someday experience such beauty, and painlessness, and tranquility. In the incredible lightness, he knew everything was okay. And he let go.

⁂

It was not until the next day that Alton was found, and fate would have it that Teri was the one who discovered him.

It was the first real argument Mother and I had; I wanted to look for my friend, but after three days of not being able to get ahold of Al, she and Teri felt something was wrong. I think she didn't want me, at fifteen, to experience something awful so she made me stay and listen for the telephone in the house. Teri had gone to Al's house and his Jeep was there, but he did not answer the door. We all knew that he preferred to walk somewhere to fish, and the closest place was Dibbin Creek. They would check there. If they did not find him, Teri planned to break in and check his house.

She and Teri checked the cabin and there was no sign of him. Then Mother walked upstream toward the faster water where the trout live, and Teri walked downstream. Both calling out his name at the top of their lungs.

Weaving through the alders and fern along the creek bank, Teri had to walk only two hundred yards. She brushed some alder branches away from her face and saw him. Al looked like he was napping against the tree. She screamed, "Al!? … ALTON!?"

Teri lunged forward and checked Al's pulse. There was none. He was cold as ice. She stood back for a moment, staring at Al from a few feet away, then bent to the left and threw up. She ran, crying, back to the cabin and beyond the cabin farther upstream until she could clearly hear Rachel yelling Al's name.

"RACHEL!"

"TERI?"

Mother sprinted back downstream and hugged Teri who was weeping, trying to speak. Mom knew. With tear-filled eyes she asked, "Where is he?"

Teri's throat hurt so much it was difficult to speak. "Just past the cabin." She took a deep breath. "Under an old cedar tree."

They held each other for a couple of minutes, then walked slowly together toward the cabin. Once there, they collected themselves.

"Okay," Mother said. "I'll go call the sheriff, but I want to cover him up." She stopped and fetched from the cabin the old horse blanket that Sam had used for a bedsheet when he built his first shelter.

"I'll go do it," Teri offered.

But Rachel could see in Teri's face that she was only being brave. "Actually, Teri, we're in no hurry. Let's go together. When I go back to call the police, I'll have to tell Sam, and if you don't mind I'd like you to be with me. We both should tell him."

Teri, still crying, nodded and hugged Rachel again. "He's this way …"

Alton looked peaceful, leaning against the tree. He looked like he was asleep. Both arms rested in his lap, his hands on his thighs palms-up. His hat, tilted back, was somehow still on his head. Teri combed Al's hair back a little with her fingers and straightened the hat. They covered his head down to his knees with the old blanket.

Rachel noticed the fly rod on the creek bank. The line was still in the water. She picked it up to bring it up to the house and when she did she realized there was a fish still on the line. It had gotten tangled in some weeds and sticks over the last many hours, but it was still alive. Rachel managed to strip the fish in and, still alive, untangle it and release it.

The two women walked very slowly back up the tractor trail to the house. They walked silently, holding hands. As they walked past the barn, Teri finally said, "He's going to struggle with this."

They stepped onto the driveway and saw me sitting on the porch holding a book. The door to the kitchen was open so I could hear the telephone. I saw Mother and Teri coming, and I saw their faces. I stood up before they got to the steps. By the time they climbed the top step, I knew. The book fell to the porch and I put my head in my hands and started crying. It was a low, choking cry coming right from my gut and my throat hurt. Both women held me and each other simultaneously.

I started sobbing uncontrollably. Teri rubbed my back. "Here," Mother said, guiding each of us to sit on the step. A minute or two went by until Mother finally said, "Oh, Honey. It'll be all right. He loved you very much."

"I know," I said in a high-pitched voice through tears and snot. "I just … I'm going to miss him so much." That set Teri off again and now Mother and I comforted her.

For an hour, we cried and consoled each other.

At the first moment we all three had stopped crying and were catching our breaths, Mother offered, "You'll be glad to know Al had a fish on when he went. A big bass."

"That's good," I sniffed. I took a very deep breath. "What do we do now?"

"We have to call the sheriff," Mother replied, "and they'll come get him. There will be a funeral in a few days. I'm sure he left directions in a will or something that will tell what he wanted to be done."

"I think I want to see him," I said.

Teri and Mother looked at each other. Teri shrugged at Mother who asked, "Are you sure?"

I nodded. "Is he—I mean, is he in the water or anything?"

"No, Honey." Mother brushed my hair with her fingers and smiled. "No, no. He looks like he's napping under a big cedar tree. He looks peaceful, like he's resting."

I mustered a tear-soaked smile.

"What do you think Teri?" Mom asked.

"This is all you," she replied.

"No, we're a family. I want to know if you think he should."

Teri nodded slowly. "Then I think he should if he wants to.

I had calmed down a great deal but was still processing what was happening.

Teri held my face, looked me in my eyes, and spoke slowly. "I've seen you make amazing strides, Sam, in the past two years. Alton gave you many gifts: the gifts of fly fishing, fly tying, a better appreciation of biology, conservation, cabin construction, self-confidence, humility, and most importantly, the gift of reading. We all knew Alton. I think he would want you to face this with a natural spirituality and maturity, with an understanding that this is the way life goes, and he'd want you to hold onto his generous gifts and focus on them. Sam, Al told me once that he loved that you are an honest, kind, boy who is mature beyond your years. You can honor him now by remembering his gifts and growing up into an honest, kind, man."

We did not call the authorities right away. All three of us walked back to the creek. Mother and Teri sat a ways back and gave me some private moments with Al. They watched from that safe distance as I touched my forehead to Al's and then covered him again with the blanket.

I walked back to the two women in my life as they pushed themselves to their feet. Teri would tell me years later that walking up the trail, I looked older than a fifteen-year-old, and that I carried myself differently, but she never said how.

Then Mother called the sheriff.

Thirty
THY WILL BE DONE

Months later, while Sam was at school, Rachel was washing the breakfast dishes when she heard a truck roll slowly down the driveway. It sounded a little like Alton's old Willey's Jeep, and a wave of sadness washed over her as she moved to the window to look. Down the driveway, nearer to the seldom-used front door, was parked a new-looking pickup truck. A tall, fit, nicely dressed man was walking to the front door. He carried a briefcase under his arm.

Insurance man? she thought. *They stopped coming here years ago…*

Rachel quickly untied her apron, threw it onto the back of one of the kitchen chairs, and dried her hands some more as she walked through the living room to the front of the house. She arrived at the door as the man knocked.

"May I help you?"

"Yes, ma'am. If you are Rachel Candage." She felt uneasy.

"My name is David Ashe. I'm from the offices of Diebold, Nasberg, & Oldham in Springfield."

Rachel just looked at him and took a deep breath. She nodded.

"We have an office here in Milton," Mr. Ashe offered.

There was an awkward moment as Mother's mind started to race. *What is this?* she thought. *What now?*

"Would it be okay if we stepped inside?" Ashe asked.

Rachel turned her head and looked at the truck in the driveway. It had been turned around and was parked facing the road. A teenage boy was sitting in the driver's seat, and she could see he was reading a book.

"Yes, of course. Sorry..."

Rachel showed the man into the front room. Her mind got away from her. *Am I getting served?* she thought. She looked down at the end of the driveway. *Did someone fall at the flower stand and break their wrist? Oh God! Was there some weird back tax issue with the farm I don't know about? Are we going to lose the farm?!*

They both sat, Rachel in the first chair she came to and Mr. Ashe on the end of the couch closest to her. Ashe, without a smile, reached out his hand and said, "It's nice to meet you."

Rachel felt sick to her stomach. She shook his hand feebly.

Ashe felt it and saw her worried look. He held onto her hand a few seconds longer than normal and said, "Mrs. Candage, everything is all right. There's nothing wrong." He let go of her hand.

Rachel exhaled and mustered a slight smile. She retracted her hand and sat back in her chair. Ashe sat forward on the edge of the couch.

Rachel said, "I thought maybe...well, what can I do for you then, Mr. Ashe?"

Ashe removed the briefcase from his lap and placed it on the couch beside him. He remained leaning forward and clasped his fingers together, almost as if praying.

"This is going to be a lot for you to take in and will take fifteen to twenty minutes," he said. "Do you have the time now to talk?" He did not want to start stating his business only to get halfway through.

"I have the time." Rachel was very curious now.

"Fine. First, I think you should know that I knew your husband—and Mr. Sands. Not professionally, I fished with both of them up on the Sebatekew River. Only a few times with Jody, but, like most people, I became enamored with Alton, and I would often try to fish with him or near him. It was a wonder to watch him cast a fly."

"Yes," Mother offered. "We loved Alton."

Ashe smiled and nodded at her. "Anyway, I think it's because we fished together some that he came to me."

Rachel sat, waiting for Ashe to continue.

The attorney hesitated, then continued. "Mrs. Candage, Alton came to me last year for his estate planning."

Rachel slumped a little in her chair. She still grieved for Alton, and her emotions had been up and down for weeks. Now, it appeared that perhaps Alton had left her something in his will. Or maybe to Sam. She fought back tears. Mr. Ashe recognized her discomfort and gave her a moment. He paused and looked around the room. He saw by the construction of the fireplace that it was a very old house. He noticed the grandfather clock and the pictures on the walls.

"I met with Alton several times to go over his affairs," he continued. "He and Alice had no children, and there are no living heirs."

Ashe leaned his head forward to make sure she was focused, and Rachel looked squarely at him.

"Mr. Sands had hoped there would be sufficient funds to cover any mortgage that might exist on the farm."

Rachel, dumbfounded, continued to stare into Mr. Ashe's eyes.

"Mrs. Candage, Alton left the entire estate to you and Sam," he said. "It's a substantial amount."

Rachel held her hand over her mouth. Again, he gave her a few seconds to grasp what he was saying.

"Upon liquidation of the estate, which includes his home and three other properties, $60,000.00 will be set aside for a college fund for your son, and there are a few specific named items to be awarded to Theresa Williams of Milton, whom I understand you are close friends with."

"Teri, yes. We are very close. And she loved Alton. She … she is the one who found him, down by the creek."

Mr. Ashe nodded. "The real estate market can fluctuate, as I'm sure you know, and we have not yet obtained bank appraisals, but our realtors have made an opinion of value for all the properties at somewhere between $350,000.00 to $400,000.00."

Rachel took a deep breath, and tears started flowing down her face. Attorney Ashe had seen such reactions many times before when people experienced life-changing events. He knew just when to pause and when to proceed. It took her a few minutes to compose herself.

Finally, she said, "This is all so unexpected." Rachel shook her head. "I'm … still grieving. We'd rather still have Alton with us."

"Of course. I understand." David Ashe did not hurry the conversation. "There are a few details we should go over, and then I'll leave you to digest this news. It's simply some administrative information. Are you ready for me to go on?"

Rachel sniffed and wiped her nose with a tissue. "I'm okay. Please, go on. Should I write this down?"

"No, Ma'am. I have an official letter for you declaring everything we talk about, including prescribed schedules. You can refer to the letter at your convenience."

"Okay," said Mother, still sniffing. She drew a deep breath.

Mr. Ashe proceeded. "I am the executor of the will, so you and I will be in contact throughout the next six months to a year. Longer if need be. You can set up an appointment through our office in Milton when we can formalize everything. Normally we summon people to our offices and give the news, but Alton asked me to personally come here to tell you in your own home, and I obviously agreed.

"Also, Alton hand-wrote letters to you, Samuel, and Ms. Williams. I'll leave yours and your son's with you. I've sent a letter to Ms. Williams asking her to pick hers up at the office."

Neither spoke for a full minute. Ashe looked around the tidy room again.

"You don't see many grandfather clocks these days," he said. "Everything's going digital." Then Ashe turned back toward Rachel. "This may be a tad unprofessional, but because of your relationship with Ms. Williams…"

"Teri," Rachel interjected.

"Teri," he continued. "I want to tell you that Alton left in his will his entire art studio contents to her. It is quite considerable."

"Al painted? I know he was artistic; he was always sketching bits of nature for us. I saved every one of them."

"Yes. He was a very good pastel and watercolor artist. And he loved the outdoors, as you know."

Rachel nodded. She had regained her composure completely.

Ashe went on as if they were now having a casual conversation. "A peculiar thing about Alton. He was a good artist, surely, but he never signed any of his work. The poetry got in the way of that."

Rachel glanced at Ashe. "What does that mean?"

Ashe's face held the slightest hint of a smile. He was not smiling—not in the least—yet it was there. Perhaps it was in his eyes.

"Whenever I saw Al on the river, I would find a boulder or a log to sit on and just watch him. It was a marvel to watch him work a river. And I loved to watch him release a salmon; there was such reverence to it. When he released a fish, Alton gently cradled it with his palms and fingers wide open. He hardly handled the fish at all."

Rachel listened to the story and realized he must be telling her this because he, too, was mourning the loss. She thought she could see the young attorney's eyes well up a little.

Ashe could see the lack of clarity on Rachel's face. This time he boldly smiled.

"You see, Mrs. Candage..."

"Rachel," she interrupted a second time. "Enough of this formality." She managed a smile of her own.

"You see, Rachel, Alton asked very little of life, and he demanded nothing from it. He was blessed with the talent to draw, paint, and teach, and that was enough for him. After his wife died, he was down, but then he found all of you, and he was so happy to give what he had in his life to you three. You were his family."

Rachel bowed her head.

"Please don't cry just yet," Ashe said.

Rachel looked up at him. That was an odd request.

Ashe stood in front of her and again clasped his hands together as if in prayer. "Al explained to me once that he didn't sign his artwork because he felt it sucked the poetry out of the piece. Cheapened it, somehow. I didn't understand it."

Rachel looked confused.

"I know," Ashe said, smiling. "We're bordering on eccentric now."

"Getting there," Rachel responded. "But Al was such a wonderful soul, whatever he chose to do or not do was fine with me."

"Agreed. Rachel, you know that Al and your husband fished together?"

"Yes, well, Alton told me he had met him on the river."

"Met him? Yes. And fished together, ate lunches together, and netted each other's fish. Some of us on the river called them kindred spirits."

Rachel sat back in her chair and sighed. "Al never said ..."

Then Ashe unclasped his hands and held them out, palms up. "What was your husband's favorite poem? Do you remember?"

"Of course. *Birches*, by Robert Frost. He loved that poem."

Ashe smiled broadly. "Come ... indulge me." He walked across the room, and Rachel followed. He turned on a floor lamp near the overstuffed chair and tilted the shade up toward the painting of Jody fishing.

After peering closely, Ashe finally said, "There, right there, in the bark of the tree." He held his finger out.

Rachel squinted, her face only inches from the painting.

Suddenly, there it was, in tiny text, written vertically from top-to-bottom in the trunk of the tree;

"One could do worse than be a swinger of birches."

Another tear slid down her cheek. She exhaled deeply, staring at the letters. "All this time. He never told us."

"I thought not." Ashe stared at the painting. "It wouldn't have been his way *to* tell you."

Ashe almost patted Rachel on the shoulder but stopped himself. "Well, I'd better get going. Left my boy out there reading. But, if I know him, by now, he's trying to get down to the creek to fish."

Rachel walked Ashe to the door. The boy was out of the truck, not fishing, but rather tossing pinecones in the air and trying to hit them with a stick, pretending to swing a baseball bat. She watched as Ashe messed his kid's hair up as they climbed into the truck.

She went back inside, took the painting off the wall, sat down in the comfortable chair, and placed the picture in her lap. *Nothing will be the same*, she thought.

Thirteen Years Later

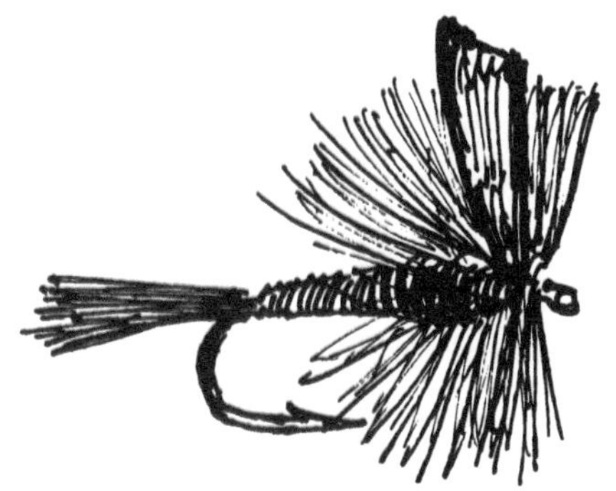

I didn't become a fly fishing guide until my twenty-sixth birthday. As a teacher, I knew I'd have time to guide during the summers. But as I drove up Route 2 and the usual memories flooded back to me, I tried to tell my girlfriend Roxanne about my crazy childhood. She well knew that my dad died when I was very young, and she knew all about my mentor Alton Sands. "He was a sage of a man," I always told her.

"As a youngster," I told 'Rocks,' while keeping both eyes on the road, "I spent an extraordinary amount of time simply thinking, especially as I approached my teens. There may have been too much thinking. I bet some of it was just boredom. Lacking playmates, it was always only me, and whenever I exhausted all the things I could come up with to do on my own, I would think about life, nature, death, or the future. I wasn't trying to think about such things. They just showed up on their own. I imagine it's the same for all pre-teens. Little did I know then that it's nearly impossible to capture those feelings or ideas and turn them into something useful. They were unsought, unsortable thoughts. Usually, they showed up without warning, quickly, like a damselfly darting by, and just as quickly, my thoughts turned as usual to fishing. I truly loved to fish. And as you know, I still do."

"Well," said Rocks, "I think you turned out pretty well." She leaned across the console of my Jeep and kissed my cheek.

"Can't wait to show you the cabin."

I swung into the driveway and parked in front of the porch. Teri burst out of the kitchen and ran around to the driver's side and almost tackled me as I got out.

"Oh, I'm so glad to see you!"

"Love you, Teri," I said. I reached my arm out. "And this is Roxanne. I call her Rocks, but spelled, R, o, c, k, s, not Rox."

Teri had already embraced Rocks and they hugged and liked each other right away. "That spelling sounds about right," Teri whispered to her. "Sam likes to be a little different sometimes, but whatever he comes up with is usually pretty cool."

I chimed in. "In every childhood picture of Rocks, she's playing with dirt or stones."

"You're the artist!" Rocks said.

"I try," Teri said. Then she made a loud click with her cheek and tongue and looked pensively at Roxanne. "Can I *please* call you Rocks? I really love that name."

"Of course. I've gotten used to it over the past eight months."

Teri slapped my shoulder. "Your mom's at the cabin, spring cleaning. Let's walk down and surprise her."

The tractor path to the cabin had been improved to a real road some years before. As we passed the pumpkin field, I saw a couple of teenagers walking along the plastic mulch, sowing seeds. *We never could've afforded hiring help years ago*, I thought.

The farm looked great, well-kept, and clean ... it looked pretty. Something caught my eye in the sky. I noticed two tree swallows swooping and climbing into the blue. I tried to see if they were playing with a feather, but they were too far away.

"What has Sam told you about the cabin?" Teri asked.

Rocks answered, "Just that he and Alton built it when he was a teenager, and that now it's an artist's and writer's studio in the summer."

"That's right. It's offered as a retreat each July and September, the best months for it.

"We had electricity put in a few years ago. The writers wanted it because most of them use electric typewriters these days. So, Ed LeBlanc in Milton organized a few guys he knew and they all volunteered and dug a ditch all the way from the house and laid in wires."

The three passed the gate and turned the corner at the creek. "Here it is," Sam said, stretching out his arm.

"Oh, it's beautiful!" Rocks said. "Sam, you didn't tell me how lovely it is. I love the stained glass window—oh, there are two of them!"

Rocks noticed the wooden sign over the door: "**Alton's Holt**"

"Those stained glass windows are Rachel's," Teri offered. "She's very good. She just got commissioned to make a window for the State House."

"You don't say," I said.

Teri yelled as they reached the steps. "Hello, the house!"

We could hear Mother exclaim and scurry to the door. It swung open and she jumped out into my arms.

"Mom—Mom, this is Roxanne."

"Rocks," said Teri, grinning. "With a *ck*, not an *x*.

"I'm so glad to meet you, Mrs. Candage."

"Ha! Rachel, please." Mother hugged Rocks almost as much as Teri had.

Roxanne felt very much at home.

"Come, come," Mother said. "See the cabin."

As they all entered the cabin, I stopped on the porch. "Mom, give me a couple of minutes, while you show Rocks the cabin?"

"Sure, Honey."

Rocks moved to go with me, but Teri smiled and touched her on the shoulder. "He'll be right back." Then Teri winked. They went inside. As I walked downstream, I heard Teri tell Rocks, "A holt is an otter's den. Alton liked otters and he used to watch a pair from this cabin's porch."

I got to the big cedar tree and sat down and leaned my back against it. I reached up and pulled a cedar sprig from a bough and smelled it. I inhaled deeply, slid down the tree, sat down, and then spoke aloud.

"Sorry I've been gone for over a year, Al. There's lots going on. Let's see, teaching is going well, and I've signed up for two more classes. I'm going to get certified to teach special ed. I know you'd like that.

"But here's the big news … I've got a girlfriend now; can you believe that? She's beautiful, sweet, and easy going. *And* she fly fishes. She's a teacher also. Her name is Roxanne. Mom and Teri are showing her your cabin right now.

"Anyway, I'm going to ask her to marry me, my friend. I don't know that she's anything like Alice, but I do know you'd love her. I haven't mentioned anything about proposing to anyone else. I wanted you to know first.

"I also want you to know that I'm teaching a fly fishing course at the school. There are nine boys and three girls in the class. One of the youngest of the boys is in the autism spectrum, and I think the class is really helping him. I've volunteered to tutor him after class, and I often think of you whenever we make a breakthrough. I wouldn't be in a position to help those kids if it wasn't for you.

"All right; that's all for now. I love you, Al, and I miss you."

I got up and looked out over Dibbin Creek. The late afternoon sun washed the alders and cedars with a soft, golden light. A few fish rose and broke the surface of the pool and a damselfly zipped by and alighted on a nearby fern. I suddenly could see with perfect clarity a late afternoon I had spent on the creek with Alton over a decade ago, when a mayfly hatch clouded the sky with the flittering, delicate flies. I smiled as I remembered Al explaining the mating ritual that was about to take place high above the creek. I turned from the tree and scanned the water for otters but didn't see any. Then I cleared my throat, took a big, deep breath—then another, and walked back upstream.

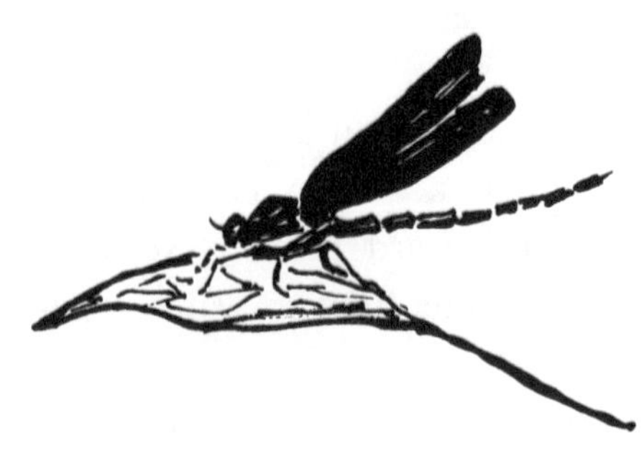

ACKNOWLEDGMENTS

Writing books, as it turns out, is very hard. It helps immensely when you have the help and support of family, friends, and other writers and creators. My siblings are always supportive, as are my wife Lisa, daughter Sam, and son Hazen, who helps with editing and tries to keep me clear-eyed.

I'm always thankful for my stable of First Readers: Monica Coffey (there only in team spirit for this one—but that counts), Laurie Marcotte, Hazen Dauphinee, Cheryl Daigle, Alan Comeau, Brian Folster, John Holyoke, and Bonnie Galayda. Many thanks to editor Anne Nelson for her fine work and diligence. Special thanks to Cyrus Wraith Walker, who always comes through and has the patience of Job.

My agent, Paul Lucas, at Janklow & Nesbit Literary Agency, has my thanks. He doesn't rep fiction, but he always answers emails and phone calls, offering expert advice, and that's worth a mention in any book, fiction or not.

ABOUT THE AUTHOR

Denis "Dee" Dauphinee

Dee is an American author of novels, biographies, and essays. His writing has gained a following with readers interested in the out-of-doors, human interest, history, travel, and fly fishing. He has been a mountaineering and fly fishing guide, a photographer, a farmer, an orthopedic physician's assistant, and a semi-pro football wide receiver.

Dee split his time between Jackson Hole, WY, New England, and Vancouver, British Columbia, for over a decade. He has led or co-led mountaineering, desert, and jungle expeditions on 5 continents. His guiding and photography took him to El Salvador, Peru, the Arctic, Europe, Nicaragua, Venezuela, Iraq, Israel, Egypt, Ecuador, Jordan, the UK, Panama, Africa, and many places in between doing photographic spec work for several media outlets, including United Press International. Now he writes about those places.

Dee lives in Middle Maine.

Other Books by Dee:

Stoneflies and Turtleheads

The River Home

Highlanders Without Kilts

When You Find My Body:
The Disappearance of Geraldine Largay
on the Appalachian Trail

All the Creatures that Breathe

ENDNOTE REVIEW REQUEST

If you enjoyed reading this, please leave a review on your social media or news outlets. I read many reviews, and they help new readers discover my books. Also, if you're interested in my giveaways or reading my occasional blog pieces or newsletters, please sign up for correspondence at: https://www.ddauphinee.com/contact.

Many thanks! — Dee

www.ingramcontent.com/pod-product-compliance
Lightning Source LLC
Chambersburg PA
CBHW030534310726
48979CB00010B/1901/J

* 9 7 8 0 9 8 6 3 0 8 9 7 0 *